NURSE, NANNY…
BRIDE!

CHAPTER ONE

So this was what it felt like to faint.

As if a plug had been pulled out of your brain and all the blood was disappearing in a rush to leave a curious buzzing sensation in its wake.

Alice tried to move her feet but they were lead weights. Just as well she could still move her arm. Catching hold of the metal rail along the side of one of the few empty beds in this emergency department was her best chance of remaining upright.

'Are you okay, Ally?' The voice of the nurse lowering the rail on the other side of the bed seemed to be coming from a very long way away. 'You've gone as white as a sheet.'

'I…' Alice was gripping the rail as if her life depended on it. The black spots interfering with her vision were starting to fade. Any second now and she would be able to take a second look. She must have been mistaken, surely? It couldn't possibly really be Andrew Barrett standing on the other side of this department. He was a world away. In London. A world she'd been only too happy to leave behind in the end.

'Sit!' Strong hands were guiding Alice towards the chair beside the bed. The one the patient's relatives usually sat on. 'Sit down and put your head between your knees.'

Alice resisted the pressure. 'I'm okay, Jo.'

She was. The buzzing was gone. Blood was reaching her brain again almost as fast as it had left, thanks to the increase in her heart rate. 'I'm just a bit...'

Shocked. Slapped by a reminder of a past she had worked very hard to escape from. It probably wasn't even him. Just someone who looked a bit like him from the side. Tall and well built with slightly scruffy dark blond hair and the weathered skin of a man who loved to be outdoors. A figure familiar enough to push a lot of old buttons.

Bright ones like desire.

Much darker ones such as envy.

'Exhausted?' Jo supplied. 'I'm not surprised. What time did you get back home last night?'

'About eleven, I guess.'

'And how long was the drive?'

'More than ten hours. Mostly thanks to the radiator boiling with my old truck trying to pull a horse float over the pass.'

'Oh, no! You poor thing. I'll bet it took an hour or more to offload Ben and get things sorted when you got home, too. You probably haven't had more than a few hours' sleep and that's on top of a week of having to sort your gran's property and everything.' Jo's arm came around Alice in a swift hug. 'Have you even had any breakfast, hon?'

'No.' In fact, it was hard to remember when she'd last

had a proper meal. No wonder she'd nearly fainted. Or was imagining things. The swirl of disturbing emotions was still there. Making her stomach feel a shade queasy.

'Go into the staff room right now and make yourself some toast. And hot chocolate. I'll tidy up in here.'

Again, Alice shook her head. The route to the staff room would mean having to brush past the two men who were peering at one of the wall-mounted X-ray screens on that side of the department. And maybe she hadn't been imagining things. Maybe one of those men was someone she hadn't expected and really didn't want to see. Ever again. It would be too hard going down that particular road again. Negotiating painfully bumpy terrain that led absolutely nowhere.

'I'm fine now, really.' Alice smiled. She was. She could move again. She lowered the rail on the bed and tugged at the sheet that needed changing. 'And it was worth all the hassle. I couldn't have left Ben for more than a week when there was nobody to keep an eye on him and the beach rides more than made up for the stress of having to clean out Gran's place. The last tenants made a hell of a mess. It's no wonder it barely sold for enough to cover the mortgage.'

'At least it's settled.' Jo was moving back to the other side of the bed as Alice rolled up the sheet and stuffed it into the linen bag. 'Having to pay that on top of your rent for the last year's been a killer, hasn't it?'

Alice nodded. There was nothing she could say. It had just been one of those things. It had to be done so she'd done it. The same way she had dealt with all the hard stuff that life had a habit of dumping her in. Head on. Standing tall. Fainting was definitely not an option.

Alice took a deep breath and deliberately shifted her gaze. She was ready to get her bearings.

'Who *is* that?' she asked calmly. 'Talking to Peter?'

Jo glanced over her shoulder. When she turned back to Alice, her eyebrows were a little higher and a smile tugged at one corner of her mouth. 'Andy Barrett. New consultant. Cute, huh?'

Alice couldn't say anything. Hopefully Jo wouldn't interpret her stare as anything more than curiosity.

'He's English. Started work here the day after you left last week. We were all surprised. Turns out that Dave had health issues he didn't want anyone to know about and finding his replacement had been kept well under wraps. Apparently we really scored getting this Dr Barrett. He's been the head honcho at some big London hospital for years. Can't remember which one. Hammersmith, maybe.'

Alice couldn't trust herself to open her mouth. If she did she might tell Jo that it hadn't been Hammersmith. It had been the same hospital she had worked in herself for over a year.

Until she'd been as good as fired.

By one Dr Andrew Barrett.

Jo didn't know any of that story. No one here did and that was exactly the way Alice wanted it to be. No way was she getting pulled back anywhere near that black period of humiliation again. Not now. Apart from the death of her grandmother a year ago and the ten days leave she had just taken to sort out the eventual sale of the isolated cottage the only remaining member of her family had lived in, Alice's life was finally on track again.

She was still staring at the profile of the man who presented a new and very unwelcome threat. Both professional *and* personal.

Why had he come all the way to the opposite side of the earth and picked the one place that was hers? It wasn't as if New Zealand was *that* small. He could have picked one of the larger cities in the north island. Maybe they didn't have as many ski fields or mountains to climb but they had plenty of water. He could have learned to sail. Or surf!

Maybe Pam would know why. Contact with the only friend she had kept from her time in London was well overdue and if what she was seeking was the kind of gossip she deliberately avoided, so be it. Knowledge was power and Alice certainly needed a boost.

Just making the decision to email Pam gave Alice the illusion of regaining some control. About to drag her gaze away from the new member of staff, she only just caught the movement as he raised his left hand to indicate something of interest on the image.

Unaware of the frown on her face, she turned to help Jo smooth and tuck fresh linen onto the bed. The last time she had seen Andy Barrett he had been wearing a wedding ring. A tight band of gold that had successfully suffocated any stupid fantasies she might have nurtured.

He wasn't wearing it now.

The case in Resus 1 was a trauma. A thirty-five-year-old woman who was well known to emergency department staff: one of their 'frequent flyers'. Her boyfriend had gang affiliations and was only too ready to use his fists and his feet when something displeased him, but

Janine had steadfastly refused to lay any complaints against him on earlier visits. Maybe this time would be different, the triage nurse told the consultant. It was the worst punishment they'd ever seen her receive.

Janine lay, oddly quiet, on the bed, her face now so swollen it was obviously painful for her to speak.

'No!' she managed in response to Andrew's careful suggestion. 'No police. I told you. I fell down the stairs.'

Yeah…right. Stairs that had knuckles and heavy boots. The lacerations on her eyebrow and upper lip needed extensive suturing. A cheekbone was probably fractured and Andrew didn't like the ugly purple bruises already appearing on her ribs as a nurse cut away her clothing.

'Can you take a deep breath for me?' Andrew was using both hands to examine her ribs as gently as he could.

'Ahhh!' It was the first indication Janine had given of her level of pain.

'Pretty sore, isn't it?' Her breathing was adequate but unsurprisingly shallow. 'What score would you give it on a scale of one to ten, Janine? Ten being the worst.'

'I'm all right.' Janine sounded as if she was holding her breath now. She had her eyes closed and beads of perspiration mingled with the blood on her forehead. She was a long way from being all right.

'Anything else hurting that much?'

A tear escaped puffy eyelids. 'My…arm, I guess.'

The sleeve of a ragged jersey was being peeled away and the deformity of Janine's wrist and lower arm was obvious. Another fracture. Almost open. Andrew could see the bone just under the skin. Checking limb baselines like movement and sensation and perfusion seemed inadvisable until the fracture was secured. Even trying to wriggle her fingers might be enough to break the skin and risk infection. He turned to the nurse and lowered his voice.

'She didn't come in by ambulance, did she?'

Jo shook her head. 'Private car. She was left outside Reception to make her own way inside.'

Andrew's mouth tightened as he shook his head in disgust. He had to bury the anger that might have made him storm out of here if the bastard was hanging around. He had to rid his head of the ugly words he would like to have said to the kind of man who could treat a woman like this.

And, most of all, he had to dismiss the memory of what it felt like to be suspected of being that kind of man. 'Let's get an IV line in and a splint on this arm,' he ordered crisply. 'We'll get some pain relief on board and then do a thorough secondary survey before we start the X-rays.'

Another nurse entered the resuscitation area as Andrew slipped a tourniquet around Janine's arm and tightened it. 'I'm going to put a small needle in your hand,' he warned his patient. 'Then we can give you something for the pain. Okay?'

Janine nodded. The movement made her wince. In his peripheral vision, as he anchored a vein and slipped a cannula into place, Andrew could see the new nurse sliding a well padded cardboard splint under Janine's broken arm and then starting to secure it. Her movements were sure and careful enough not to cause further damage or pain.

He taped the cannula and looked up properly this time, intending to let the nurse know that she'd done a good job. It was just as well he hadn't done this a few seconds ago. He might have missed the vein completely.

Alice Palmer?

He'd known she came from New Zealand. Why had it not even occurred to him that she might be working in a hospital here again? Because the odds of it being the same one he'd been offered a job in by an old acquaintance were so small? Or was it because he'd been so determined to put any thoughts of her and the period of his life she'd been a part of completely behind him?

How ironic that he'd come *this* far to get away from it all. To start again and here it was, staring him in the face. Right beside a case that graphically represented most of what he'd been trying to escape.

He stared back.

How much did Alice know? Not much, presumably, because she'd lost her job before it had started. Unfair dismissal, as it had turned out. And he'd been responsible. He had had every intention of telling her, but when he'd gone to the address the woman in Personnel had given, he'd found an empty house with a 'For Sale' sign outside that had a cheerful 'Sold' sticker planted in the centre. It had been six months after the event, in any case, and someone in Emergency had suggested that Alice had left the country.

He couldn't tell her now. It was ancient history and here she was, working in a senior position so it hadn't affected her career. And if he did tell her, she'd want to know how he knew and that was what had had to be left behind.

For Emmy's sake.

He held her gaze and kept his tone carefully neutral as his brain worked overtime, tossing up whether to acknowledge the fact that they knew each other.

'I'd like some morphine drawn up, please,' he said.

No. He couldn't acknowledge her. That would bring a flurry of interest from others. Questions he didn't want to hear, let alone answer. His next words emerged before he'd had a chance to even think them through. A form of attack as a defensive shield.

'If you have keys to the drug cabinet, that is.'

Heat scorched Alice's cheeks.

She dragged her eyes away from his face. An older-looking face. Thinner and far more distant. Had he changed so much from the man she remembered or was this coolness due to a determination to hide recognition? So this was how it was going to be. They were not going to acknowledge having worked together, let alone knowing what they did know about each other.

A warning shot had been fired. If she said anything about the rumours she'd been hearing before she left London, he would warn her superiors that allowing her access to restricted drugs might be inadvisable.

The unfairness of it added a new element to the emotional turmoil Alice was dealing with. Despite the traitorous reaction of her body earlier, she knew she wasn't in love with the man any more. She'd got over that a very long time ago. About when she'd been standing in front of his desk and he'd said he couldn't trust her enough to let her keep the job she loved.

She'd tried to hate him for that but hadn't succeeded.

Her heart had been incapable of flipping the coin to embrace the dark side of love. Especially when her head, coupled with an innate sense of fairness, had forced her to acknowledge that he'd only been doing what he had to do as head of department. Quite generously, really, when he'd offered her the opportunity to resign instead of launching an official investigation and a paper trail that would have haunted the rest of her working life.

What was really unfair was that she'd never believed the rumours about *him*. Even now, with the dark emotions sparked by seeing the poor battered woman they were treating at the moment and the cool distance he had placed between himself and an old colleague, she knew he was as incapable of hurting someone deliberately as she was of stealing and taking drugs. If Andrew had been interested enough to actually get to know her properly, he would have had—would still have—the same kind of faith in her.

Clearly, he didn't. The implication beneath his request for morphine had been a deliberate reminder of the humiliating rumours she'd been unable to disprove. That he hadn't trusted her. That he'd never really seen who she was. That hurt.

Quite apart from being an intimately personal slight, mud had a habit of sticking. Enough to ruin lives. Alice actually felt sick to her stomach as she pulled an ampoule of morphine from the cabinet and signed the register. She could feel Andrew watching her.

Jo did the drug check with her. The name of the drug. The dose. The expiry date. She watched as Alice snapped the top of the ampoule and slid a needle in to draw it up. Try as she might, Alice couldn't disguise the subtle trembling of her hands.

'You still need toast,' Jo whispered.

Alice needed something a lot more than food. She needed to be a long way away from their new consultant. How could she possibly work with him when he was watching every move she made? Knowing that, despite the best of intentions and for very different reasons, she would have to fight the desire to watch every move he made? Looking for a reminder of the man she remembered. Hoping not to find one, possibly, so she could decide it had been a lucky escape and move on, once and for all.

She could switch departments, she thought wildly. Go into Cardiology. Or Paediatrics. Or Theatre. No. This was where she loved to work. Where she got a taste of everything and the adrenaline rush of helping to deal with major, life-threatening situations. This department was a big part of why her life was on track again.

She drew up the saline to dilute the morphine. She taped the ampoule to the barrel of the syringe to identify its contents and then she walked back to the bed to hand it to Andrew.

Watching Janine relax as the effect of the narcotic took the edge off her pain had a curiously similar effect on Alice. She eyed the bruised and swollen face of the woman again. The marks of brutality on the woman's ribs and the misshapen arm now resting in a splint. The thought of someone enduring a beating like this was horrific. Sickening. Alice raised her gaze, knowing that her reaction would be evident in her eyes.

Deliberately capturing the gaze of Andrew Barrett before that reaction dimmed.

Maybe she hadn't believed any of it but allowing

Andrew to think she might have was possibly the only defence she had.

They both had something they didn't want their colleagues to know. Things they didn't want to lose. Alice was more vulnerable. She had something she didn't want Andrew to know, as well. It was good that he'd chosen not to acknowledge her. Distance was safe and, if it stopped being safe, then she was prepared to fight, if that was what it would take to protect herself.

Andrew's gaze was steady. So was he, it told her.

For the moment at least, this appeared to be a stand-off.

This was a disaster.

Alice clearly knew a lot more than he would have expected. Was she still in touch with old friends in London? People who would be only too happy to gossip about a police investigation involving a consultant emergency physician? That she knew too much was as unfortunate as knowing he was perpetuating a lie by letting her think he still believed the worst of her. But what else could he do?

He'd come this far and had found what appeared to be the perfect place for himself and Emmy. They'd only been here for a little over a week but he'd never seen his daughter so happy. He knew he'd made the right decision despite how hard leaving had been. Running away from it all had gone against the grain so hard it had been painful. An admission of defeat that some would probably interpret as guilt, but he'd done it for his daughter. He wasn't going to let his little girl grow up anywhere within reach of a tainted past.

He couldn't keep running. The world of medicine was surprisingly small and, no matter where you went, someone always knew someone else. Look at the way Dave had contacted him about the possibility of this position when they hadn't seen each other since a short stint in an American hospital together ten years ago.

Andrew was between a rock and a hard place, here. Damned by his conscience whichever way he turned. The unwanted distraction filled his mind as he waited for Janine's X-ray views to appear on the screen in front of him. Should he follow his first instinct and simply talk privately to Alice? Tell the truth and then apologize? Lay his cards on the table and ask for her help?

Why would she want to do that? She'd not only lost her job. When he'd heard that she'd left the country, he'd also heard that the sale of her house had been forced by the bank. That she'd lost everything. He could have talked to her then. Tried to make amends, even, but nobody had seemed to know where she'd gone. And then the real trouble had started and he'd forgotten everything other than trying to survive. To keep Emmy safe.

What could he say now? An excuse that he couldn't have simply taken her word for her innocence and an apology for any inconvenience caused was hardly going to clear the air. It might actually make her jump at the chance for revenge.

The notion was jarring. It didn't fit with the Alice Palmer he remembered from five years ago. The attractive, competent nurse working in his emergency department. A young woman doing her O.E. who'd made friends with his fiancée. Who'd come to their wedding, in fact. She'd been good at her job. Caring. The evi-

dence that she'd been stealing morphine and other restricted drugs had been shocking. Unbelievable, really,
but you never knew with women. Look at how things
with Melissa had turned out.

Oh, *God*... No! Andrew rubbed his temple and then
raked his fingers through his hair. He didn't want to
think about Mel. Or London. Or any of what had been
left behind and that was why working with Alice Palmer
was a complication he didn't know how to resolve.

Images began appearing on the wall-mounted computer screen. It was a relief to focus as he scrolled
through them. The cheekbone probably needed wiring.
The nasty fragmented fracture of the radius and ulna
would require surgery. Orthopaedics were on the way
and someone from plastic surgery should be contacted
to deal with the facial suturing that could be done in
Theatre as well. Andrew turned back to Resus 1. He had
a job to do here. His patient needed care. And protection. A delicate situation when he couldn't know
whether it might make things worse for Janine by en-
couraging her to lay a complaint about her boyfriend.

Alice would be in Resus 1 as well. Another delicate
situation and Andrew needed more time to try and
figure out what he was going to do about it. Maybe he
could buy time by putting some distance between them.
Adjust his shifts, perhaps, so they spent as little time as
possible in the department together?

No. Why should he have to do that? He was a senior
consultant in this department now and he needed to
start the way he intended to carry on. Alice was a nurse.
A very good nurse, probably, but as far as a balance of
power went, it was weighted firmly on his side. An ad-

vantage that Andrew couldn't afford not to use. He needed to take control and make sure he kept it.

The department was relatively quiet for a long time after Janine had been taken to Theatre. Downright boring, really. Alice was looking after an epileptic man who was sleeping off the post-ictal phase of his seizure, a diabetic patient from a rest home who needed her insulin dose adjusted and another very elderly incontinent woman, Miss Stanbury, who was still suffering the effects of a gastric disturbance and needed rehydrating and frequent changing.

When an ambulance brought in a forty-year-old man with a markedly accelerated heart rate, Alice was more than ready to take on the case.

'This is Roger,' the paramedic told her. 'Narrow complex tachycardia. Rate 196. Oxygen saturation ninety-eight per cent. No cardiac history.'

Roger looked pale and frightened but he wasn't in the kind of danger he would have been in if the spikes on his ECG were wide enough to suggest the ventricles of his heart were in trouble. Alice enjoyed cardiology. She could read a twelve lead ECG better than most junior doctors and she particularly loved this kind of case. One where a dramatic result and relief for the patient could be provided.

'Have you got any chest pain?' she asked Roger.

He shook his head. 'I feel a bit short of breath, that's all. And I can feel my heart.'

'Have you ever felt it going this fast before?'

'No.'

Alice helped the paramedics transfer Roger to the

bed in Resus 2, where they had good telemetry facilities
to monitor his heart. She raised the back of the bed so
their patient was sitting up, which would help his breathing effort. Jo came in as she was transferring the oxygen
tubing from the portable cylinder to the overhead outlet.

'SVT,' Alice told her. 'Is Peter around?'

'No.' Another figure pushed through the curtains as
the paramedics took the stretcher out of the small area.
'I've got this case.' Andrew was holding the patient report form the ambulance crew had supplied. A long
strip of pink paper recording the cardiac rhythm en
route was attached to it and he was looking at the
monitor beside the bed as he spoke.

He introduced himself to his patient, who was still
looking alarmed.

'Am I having a heart attack?'

'It's one of the possibilities we're going to investi-
gate,' Andrew told him. 'But, so far, we're not seeing
any sign of it. Your heart's going a bit too fast to really
see what's happening so we're going to try and slow it
down for you. Try and relax.'

Roger made a sound like a strangled bark of laughter
and Andrew's smile was sympathetic.

'I know. Easy for me to say, standing on this side of
the equation, isn't it?' He touched his patient's arm. 'I
know this is scary but we're on the case and you're in
the best possible place to get things sorted.'

His smile and his touch had a visible effect on Roger,
who lay back against the pillow with a sigh and a nod.

They had a hopefully *invisible* effect on Alice.

This was a glimpse of the real Andrew. How many
times had she seen the effects of this man's words and

smile and touch? She hadn't really been aware of how nobody else quite measured up to the standards Andrew Barrett had set. Or how much she'd missed working with him.

Until now.

Andrew had turned to Jo. 'Got a straw handy?'

'Sure.'

'And grab a technician to come and do a twelve lead, will you, please?'

'I can do that,' Alice said quietly.

'Fine. Go ahead.' Andrew was pulling on gloves. 'I'll get the bloods off.'

Alice could have managed that as well, but maybe the consultants were also finding their day somewhat dull. She pulled the machine she needed from the corner and began attaching all the electrodes needed to get a complete picture of the electrical activity of Roger's heart.

Jo was cutting a short length of plastic straw.

'I want you to take a deep breath,' Andrew instructed Roger. 'Seal your lips around the straw and then blow through it as hard as you can for as long as you can.'

A valsalva manoeuvre was one of the dramatic ways to get this kind of cardiac arrhythmia to revert to normal. They all watched the monitor screen as Roger's face reddened with the effort. There was no change to the rate.

'Get your breath back,' Andrew said. 'And then we'll give it another go.'

The respite gave Alice a chance to get the twelve lead ECG. The electrodes were all in place.

'Try and keep as still as you can,' she asked Roger as she pressed the start button.

But he was too out of breath to comply and the trace was nothing like the clean image Alice had hoped for. Dammit! She screwed up the sheet of paper, hoping that Andrew wasn't watching.

'Let's try that again,' she said calmly. 'If you could manage to hold your breath for just a second or two while the machine captures a picture, that would be great.'

Roger managed but the sheet that emerged was missing several pieces of information that it should have recorded.

'You've lost a leg lead.' Andrew was probably look-ing at her with the same kind of studied neutrality his tone held. Alice felt her cheeks reddening as she pushed the sticky patch more firmly to the skin of Roger's left ankle.

This was mortifying. Such a simple task that she was more than capable of performing, but she was man-aging to make herself look completely incompetent. Worst of all, this was more important than it should have been. The old need to attract praise by being the best was so ingrained it was automatic. She still wanted to be noticed. To be *seen*. How pathetic was that?

Andrew was getting Roger to blow through the straw again so he'd be out of breath and she'd have to wait to try getting the recording again. When she did and it worked beautifully, Andrew wasn't even paying atten-tion. Peter had come in and they were discussing the next management step. Because their patient was wide awake, they couldn't use an external electrical charge to the heart to revert the rhythm unless they sedated him heavily. The better option was to try adenosine—a drug that gave the chemical equivalent of a jolt of electricity.

It usually worked a treat and Alice knew exactly what to do. The procedure was tricky because the drug had a very short time of being effective. It had to be injected into the right arm to get to the heart as fast as possible and it had to be chased along with a large bolus of saline. Two people had to work in unison and Alice had been the one to push the flush on many occasions.

A favourite task. A bit of a challenge to get the timing right; a few seconds delay and, sometimes with even the first dose, they would watch the screen and see the heart rate magically decreasing. The adenosine was drawn up. The big fifty mil syringe of saline was drawn up. There was one port of the IV line and both needles would go in at the same time.

Peter was hanging around to watch. The paramedics had come back from tidying their ambulance and they wanted to watch, too. Andrew had the adenosine in one hand, the saline in the other. It took two hands to push that flush as fast as possible so he needed a nurse. One who knew what she was doing.

'Alice is experienced,' Peter said. 'Done this a few times, haven't you, Ally?'

She nodded, aware of a wave of pleasure at the boost to her self-esteem as she moved around the head of the bed to change sides. The perfect twelve lead ECG was sitting on top of the machine she was leaving behind but it had yet to be seen. Alice was more than happy to be given an opportunity to redeem her apparent lack of competence.

But Andrew was looking at the nurse who was already standing by his side. 'Have you done this before, Jo?'

'No.'

'Nothing to it. Hold the barrel of the syringe firmly and put the base of your other thumb on the plunger. I'll inject the adenosine and as soon as you see my plunger hit the bottom, you push in the saline as fast as you can.'

Jo shot a glance at Alice, who had stopped in her tracks and was probably looking as dismayed as she felt.

Alice glanced at Peter but the head of department merely raised an eyebrow. If their new team member wanted to take the time to help staff develop their skills then he could hardly protest.

Neither could Alice, despite feeling even more mortified than she had when she'd messed up getting that ECG trace.

'You're IV qualified, aren't you?' Andrew asked Jo.

'Yes.'

'Then let's do this.'

Jo positioned herself closer to Andrew. Their gloved hands were touching. Side by side. Syringe by syringe. Of course, Jo had no trouble performing her part of the task and then everyone was looking at the monitor.

Alice heard the distinctive sigh from Roger which showed that the drug had reached its target, but she didn't wait to enjoy the potential satisfaction of seeing a successful result. Nobody noticed as she turned and quietly slipped out of the Resus area.

Alice wasn't needed in here. And she certainly wasn't wanted by the consultant in charge.

CHAPTER TWO

Not being able to afford a decent car had its advantages.

You could throw anything into the back of this ancient four-wheel drive. Dogs, saddles, dirty covers—it made no difference. You could also have your foot flat to the floor and not break the speed limit. Even if you were very angry and upset and weren't even thinking about how fast to take the corners, you were safe.

Living this far out of town had its advantages, too. You left the city well behind and could see only the green of paddocks and hills and the deep blue of a late afternoon sky. Autumn colours gilded tall poplar trees and animals grazed peacefully beneath them. Sheep and cattle and fat pet ponies. A goat on a chain was eating the long grass of someone's roadside verge.

Work was left behind along with the city and the further away Alice got, the more she could feel all the upsets of her day receding. Some time out was exactly what she desperately needed. Escape to the place she loved more than any patch of the earth she had ever discovered. Turning off the main road, she drove into a valley. Towards the end of this road was a property bordered by a river and enclosed by hills like a geographical hug. Hidden from the world and, for the moment at least, entirely hers.

The long driveway was lined by oak trees that were well over a hundred years old. Leaves drifted lazily from great heights and Alice rolled down her window to smell the season. A hint of damp moss and rich soil. A faint whiff of smoke from a bonfire on some neighbouring farm. The chimneys of the enormous old house weren't giving off any smoke, of course. Why would they, when the house had been empty for so long?

Finding new owners seemed unlikely in the short term. Who could afford a rather rundown old mansion these days when it was a good twenty minutes drive from the city? The cost of petrol alone would put people off, never mind the extensive renovations needed and the effort of keeping up a hilly property of at least fifty acres. The longer it took, the better as far as Alice was concerned. She was more than happy to be here as the only human tenant.

Alice took the fork in the driveway before she got more than a glimpse of the big house through the trees. She drove towards the river now. Towards the cottage that had once housed shearers and had been rented out a year ago to her friend, Mandy. Seeing the small weatherboard dwelling ahead of her, with her dog, Jake, guarding the front step, Alice could finally let go of everything bad the day had thrown at her.

The shock of being pulled back to a past she had thought long gone. Having the ashes of a distant one-sided romance stirred and finding it still showed a dismaying warmth. Enough of a glow to make the embarrassment of being deliberately put in her place as a less important staff member far more intense. Last, but by no means least, was the knowledge that if she wanted to keep the life she'd worked so hard to create for herself, she really would have to fight for it.

Alice climbed out of the truck and crouched to hug her dog, burying her face against his shaggy neck for a moment, feeling his whole body wag pleasure in her return. Alice let out her breath in a long sigh and she was smiling as she stood up.

'I'm home,' she said aloud. 'How good is that?'

Even better, she had a good two hours of daylight left. Time to saddle up Ben and take a gentle trek up the hills, through the forest and back to the river. Her huge black horse was getting on in years now and was probably a bit stiff after the long stint of being shut in the float yesterday. Besides, Alice couldn't think of anything she would rather do to centre herself again. The other things she needed like a good home-cooked meal and a long sleep could wait.

Climbing into soft old jodhpurs and pulling on her short leather boots dispelled any thoughts of uniforms. The smell of well cared for leather as she collected her tack from the stable put anything shiny and clinical on another planet. Best of all was the soft whinny of welcome from Ben when she went out to the paddock behind the cottage with Jake walking close enough to brush her leg.

She was wanted here. Trusted. Loved by her boys. Yeah…life was full of hard bits but it could also be very, very good and this was as good as it got.

A short time later, Alice swung herself up into the

saddle and clicked her tongue. Ben wasn't showing any sign of being stiff. He took the bit and pulled eagerly. Maybe he was thinking of that long empty paddock where the forest track ended. The gentle uphill slope that was the perfect place to stretch out into a good gallop.

Alice grinned.

Yes!

Television was so boring!

Emmeline Barrett was fed up with the squeaky cartoon voices. With a heartfelt sigh, she wriggled around to kneel on the couch backwards, her chin resting on her hands as she gazed out of the window at the green hills and blue skies that were so different from anything she'd ever known it was like being in a fairy tale.

Haylee, her new nanny, was lying on the other couch, flat on her back with cushions under her head and her cellphone against her ear as she continued yet another phone call.

'*No!* Oh, my God! She *didn't*... Oh?' A contemptuous snort followed. 'What*ever*! As if he'd be interested in *her*!'

Haylee had promised to take her for a walk this afternoon. Down to see the river or up to where the trees were thick enough to make that dark and scary patch on the hillside that never failed to give Emmy a lovely tickle inside when she looked at it.

Suddenly, she knelt bolt upright, not even noticing that the interminable phone call was ending on the other couch. Her jaw dropped as she watched a big black horse come out of the forest and start galloping up the hill. A dog was running behind and it had to be a lady riding the horse because Emmy could see long hair streaming out behind the hat she was wearing.

Was it a real fairy tale now? An enchanted forest? Could the lady be a princess? She watched until the magic horse disappeared over the top of the hill and then she climbed off the couch.

'Haylee?'

'Hmm?' The nanny's response sounded remarkably like a yawn.

'Can we go for our walk now? Please?' she added hurriedly as she remembered her manners.

'In a minute, okay?' Haylee's eyes were closed. 'I just need to rest for a bit.'

Emmy scowled. She looked back at her couch that faced the blaring television. She looked at the door which led into the big hallway with the tiny stones that made patterns on the floor. If she went all the way down, there was a really big wooden door that was probably too heavy for her to open, but, if she went the other way, she knew she would find the kitchen and that funny room full of tubs and taps that had a much smaller door. If she went past the clothes line outside that door, she might be able to find the hill.

She might be able to see that magic horse and the princess again.

Emmy looked at Haylee, whose eyes were still firmly shut.

'I'm going to the bathroom,' she announced. 'I need to go to the toilet.'

'Can you manage by yourself?'

'Of course I can.' The indignation was automatic. 'I'm *five*!'

'Cool. Come straight back.'

Emmy got to the door but then turned to watch for a moment longer. She saw the way Haylee's fingers relaxed their grip on the cellphone. Her new nanny didn't even notice when it slipped out of her grasp and bounced onto the floor.

Emmy stopped chewing her bottom lip. With her lips set in a rather determined smile, she went out of the door in search of magic.

Forty-year-old Roger was about to walk out of the door of the emergency department.

'Wait!' Andrew took another glance at the slip of paper in his hand and stepped in front of his patient.

'What for?'

But Roger took a step back towards the bed he'd recently vacated, having rested for a couple of hours after the successful management of his cardiac arrhythmia.

'I've just received the results of the last blood tests we took.'

'You said there was nothing wrong with my blood.'

'There wasn't. The first results came back with completely normal cardiac enzymes.' Andrew tweaked the curtain shut behind him and showed Roger the paper he held. 'This one, however, shows a raised TNT.'

'What does that mean?'

'It means that there's been some damage to heart tissue.'

Roger sat down on the bed. 'You mean, like a heart attack?'

'Yes. The level is low enough to suggest it's minor but we're going to need to admit you and run some more tests.'

'But…I want to go home.'

'I know,' he said sympathetically. 'I'm sorry.'

Roger wasn't the only one who wanted to go home. Andrew's shift had officially finished, but he took the time to explain things to Roger again and then he paged Cardiology and waited for the registrar to arrive so he could transfer care of this patient. Finally, he unhooked his stethoscope from around his neck, put on the pinstriped jacket of his suit and headed for the car park.

Minutes later and he could put his foot down. Just a little, because that was all it needed for a surge of power from his gorgeous new car. The powerful engine purred softly and the miles between work and home evaporated. Andrew sped past the rolling paddocks without seeing the autumn colours of the trees. He barely noticed the goat on the side of the road.

It seemed a very long time since he'd kissed Emmy goodbye this morning and he needed to get back to her. To their new home. To remind himself why they'd journeyed here from the far side of the world. To convince himself it was worth the disturbing prospect of having to work with someone who was such a tangible link to his old life.

He'd won the first round, though, hadn't he? Made it very clear that if they were to work together it would be on his terms. So why wasn't it making him feel any better about the future? Why had he been left with this kind of unpleasant aftertaste as though he was being forced not only to recognise, but to bring out a side of himself that he didn't particularly like?

Andrew slowed just a little as the car bounced over the undulations in the driveway formed by ancient tree roots. He glanced to his left at the fork and caught a metallic glimmer that begged a second look. A horse float was parked under the shelter of some trees. Good. The tenant had returned. Amanda someone, the solicitor had informed him.

Andrew needed to talk to this Amanda. To let her know that, unfortunately, he wouldn't be able to let her renew the lease on the cottage that was due to expire at the end of this month. He needed the cottage as accommodation. The agency had assured him they would be able to find a married couple who would jump at the opportunity of living here and working for him. A housekeeper-nanny and a farm manager. Free accommodation should ensure he got the best available and nothing but the best would do. If the couple had children, it would be a bonus. While he was making arrangements for Emmy to start school in the city, it was too far away to make out-of-school play dates easy. How much better would it be if she had company closer to home?

The sound of the television made Andrew frown as he let himself in through the front door of the magnificent old house. Why on earth was Emmy watching rubbish when she could be outside in the fresh air and enjoying the kind of exercise and surroundings that had been impossible in central London?

Finding the temporary nanny sound asleep on a

couch in the small sitting room that had once been a library was a shock. Andrew snatched up the remote and killed the noise, staring at the young woman in disbelief and then automatically scouring the room for evidence of something worse than being simply asleep. Empty bottles? *Syringes?* Not that it made any difference. History was still repeating itself. He had apparently left his daughter in the care of someone who wasn't competent enough to keep her safe, let alone care for her the way she deserved.

The sudden silence had been enough to wake Haylee.

'Where's Emmy?' Andrew demanded.

'She went to the loo.'

'Oh?' Andrew strode to the door, trying to calm down. 'Emmy?'

He called again but he could feel the emptiness of the house as he stood in the vast hallway. His pace increased as he checked the cloakroom under the sweeping stairway. He took the stairs two at a time to reach the gallery that overlooked the foyer. He checked Emmy's bedroom. His own room. He threw open door after door of rooms that didn't even contain any furniture yet.

'Emmy!'

Downstairs, he found Haylee standing near the kitchen, looking frightened.

'How long were you asleep for?'

'I…I'm not sure. Not long.'

Andrew brushed past her into the kitchen. Empty. Not even any sign of the pantry being raided for snacks. The old laundry was also empty. The back door was open.

'She's gone outside?' Andrew tried to quell a spark of panic. 'By herself?'

'She won't have gone far.'

'How on earth would you know that? You don't even have any idea how long you were asleep.' Anger surfaced with a vengeance. 'And how far do you think she would need to go to get into trouble? There's a *river* out there, for God's sake!'

'I—I'll help you look.' Haylee looked ready to burst into tears.

'No.' Andrew didn't spare the time to look back at the girl. She wasn't to know that he was as angry with himself as he was with her but fear overrode any habit of kindness. 'Get your things and go home, Haylee. I don't want you looking after my daughter. You're fired!'

He scanned the kitchen yard, with its clothes line and pattern of herb gardens surrounded by tall thick hedges that hadn't been trimmed in years. The gateway set under an arch of greenery was overgrown. Almost invisible and only just ajar. Quite enough of a gap for a small girl to have squeezed through, however.

Andrew wrenched the gate open further.

'Emmy!'

Good grief!

There was a small girl standing in Ben's paddock. A very pretty little girl with a mop of blonde curly hair and big blue eyes that were gazing up at her in open admiration. Awe, even.

'Jake!'

The warning was unnecessary. Her large dog had dropped to his haunches well away from the child. He put his nose on his front paws and prepared to wait patiently. Ben also seemed to realise that caution was advisable. He stopped, not even looking at the water trough beside the girl.

'Hello,' Alice said. 'Who are you?'

'Emmy.'

'Hello, Emmy. I'm Alice.'

She swung her leg over Ben's back and slid to the ground, pulling off her helmet and then grabbing the reins before Ben could think of stepping forward. This child was tiny. So fragile-looking close to Ben's fluffy dinner-plate-sized hooves. Especially in that pretty pink dress with her long white socks.

'I saw you,' Emmy said. 'From the window.'

'Oh?' Alice looked around, despite knowing perfectly well there were no windows nearby. This was getting weird.

'Are you all by yourself?'

Emmy nodded. 'Haylee's asleep. She's tired.'

Maybe Alice was too. Suffering from exhaustion. Or low blood sugar or something. Having some kind of delusional experience.

'Are you a princess?'

Definitely delusional. 'No.'

'Is he magic?'

A tiny finger was pointing at Ben. Big blue eyes were looking up. Way up at the head of her horse. Something in the child's expression was very familiar. The kind of longing she remembered from when she was that small. A longing that had become a dream of one day having her own pony.

Alice smiled. 'He's kind of magic,' she said softly.

'Because he makes good things happen. Would you like to pat him?'

Already big eyes widened dramatically and Alice could see the sudden tension in the small body. A flash of fear. She heard the deep breath Emmy sucked in and then saw a determined nod.

'Yes, please.'

Brave kid. Alice held out her hand. 'He wouldn't hurt you. He loves children.'

The diminutive hand went trustingly into hers. 'I'll lift you up,' Alice said, 'so you can reach his neck. That's the best place to pat him.'

Emmy's fingers looked tiny and very pale against Ben's black coat.

'He's big, isn't he? That's why he's called Ben. After Big Ben. That's a clock. In London.'

'I know that.' The child sounded indignant. 'I'm *five*!'

Alice was too startled to smile at the tone. She'd been chatting quietly simply to put Emmy at ease. It was only now that she registered the accent.

'Did you live in London, Emmy?'

'Yes.' Emmy was stretching up to reach Ben's mane.

'Where do you live now?'

'Here.'

She couldn't have walked from a neighbouring farm to get here by herself, surely. That left only one potential home. The big house. It was still quite a walk for a five-year-old to have made by herself. Who was Haylee? A sister? And where were the parents? Did they have no idea of the kind of hazards a property like this could present? What if she hadn't been home or Ben wasn't as gentle as he was? What about the river, for heaven's sake?

Alice would have something to say to Emmy's parents when she saw them.

'What's your last name?' she queried.

Emmy didn't answer. She was busy threading her fingers through a handful of mane.

Alice tried again. 'What's Daddy's name?'

'Daddy.'

Alice smiled. She gave up. Surely someone would come looking for the child soon enough. They were probably busy moving in right now and hadn't noticed her wandering off.

'Would you like to sit on top of Ben?'

'Yes, please.'

'You'll need to wear my hat. It's a special helmet just for people who sit on horses.'

A moment later and there she was. A little princess with blonde curls poking from beneath the helmet, sitting on the huge black horse which made her look like a pea on a pumpkin. A very happy princess. It was the first time Alice had seen the child smile and it was the *best* smile, simply radiating joy, quite contagious enough to have Alice standing there, smiling back.

They could have stayed like that for a very long time. Both totally content, but then Jake raised his head from his paws. The shaggy hair on his neck came up and he emitted a low growling sound.

And then, from some distance behind Alice, came the sound of a man's voice. A very angry man.

'What the *hell* do you think you're *doing* with my daughter?'

* * *

Emmy burst into tears.

Jake's growl reached an ominous level and was re-inforced with a loud bark.

But Alice didn't turn around. She couldn't. Not yet. Not when she'd recognised that furious voice.

By some twist of a malevolent fate, 'Daddy' was Andrew Barrett and he was closer by the moment.

Oh...*God*!

'Don't cry,' she said to Emmy. Or was she talking aloud to herself? 'It's all right.'

'Nooo!' Fat tears rolled down pink cheeks. 'Daddy's cross with me.'

'Actually...' Alice found a smile '...I think he's cross with *me*.'

Emmy's tears stopped. She stared at Alice. 'Why?'

Why, indeed? If anyone was to be blamed for anything right now, it most certainly shouldn't be Alice. She turned and had the satisfaction of seeing Andrew stopped in his tracks. Not only by the menacing form of Jake, who'd positioned himself between his mistress and the threatening man, but by the shock of recognition.

'What are *you* doing here?'

There was dawning horror on the face of her old boss and, for just an instant, Alice had the peculiar notion that he was afraid of her. Totally ridiculous, of course, but it was enough for her to dredge up some confidence.

'I live here. What are *you* doing here?'

'I own this property,' Andrew snapped. 'And you most certainly do *not* live here.'

'Yes, she does, Daddy.' Emmy gave a huge sniff. 'So does Ben.'

'Be quiet, please, Emmeline. I'm talking.'

Good grief! What kind of father was Andrew Barrett? Talking to a five-year-old this sternly made any fantasy of his parental skills evaporate into an unpleasant mist. Alice didn't like what she was seeing. Neither did Emmy, apparently. The small girl stuck out her bottom lip and scowled at her father. Andrew tried to take a step forward and Jake growled again.

'Call it off,' Andrew commanded.

Alice waited for a heartbeat. And then another. 'Jake,' she said softly. Her wonderful dog moved to sit beside her, pressed against her leg.

'And now get my daughter down from that monster.'

That was too much for Emmy. 'He's *not* a monster!' she declared. She leaned forward in the saddle and tried to wrap her arms around Ben's neck. They barely made it to the halfway mark. 'He's lovely,' Emmy said passionately. 'He's my new friend and he's a magic horse. Alice said so.'

Alice was gripping Emmy's leg, unsure of the child's balance. At the same time, she was watching the muscles in Andrew's face move. As though he was trying to digest the mutiny he was faced with and decide how he would deal with it. Or maybe he was trying to understand how this could possibly be happening.

Alice was with him on that one. This was a nightmare! Part of her brain, however, was registering the fact that Andrew wasn't punishing his daughter in any way for the contradiction. Maybe he wasn't as strict and controlling as first impressions had suggested. Or maybe he was just distracted by dealing with *her* for the moment. He didn't look indecisive any longer. He looked furious. His gaze was chilly enough to send a shiver up her spine.

'Where—precisely—do you live?'

'In the cottage.'

Andrew shook his head. 'No. The tenant in the cottage is someone called Amanda.'

Alice nodded. 'Mandy Jones. She signed a twelve-month lease but she decided to go to Italy with her boy-friend. I was already living with her so I took over the lease last October, when it still had six months to run.'

'I wasn't informed of any sub-lease.'

'We saw the solicitor. I signed a contract.'

'We'll have to see about that. Won't we?'

A horrible thought occurred to Alice. What if the contract was somehow illegal? Could Andrew simply kick her out? Where on earth would she go, with a horse and dog? She touched Jake's head with her free hand, seeking reassurance. Trying to stem the awful sinking feeling that, once again, her life was falling apart.

'Alice?'

She turned her face up to Emmy.

'I'd like to get down now, please.'

'Sure. Bring your leg over to this side and I'll help you.' Alice raised her arms and caught Emmy as she slid off the horse. Ben stood like a rock, bless him, but she held the little girl closer for just a moment when her feet touched the ground. Letting her know that she was safe. It was a long time since she'd hugged a child and her arms felt curiously empty when she let go.

Emmy patted Jake on his head and then walked towards her father. 'Come on, Daddy,' she said. 'I'm hungry and I want to go home.' She looked over her shoulder at Alice. 'Can I have another ride, please? Tomorrow?'

'Um…you'll need to talk to your daddy about that.'

A discussion that was unlikely to give Emmy what she wanted, judging by the look Alice was receiving from Andrew right now. If she'd felt unwanted in Resus this afternoon when he'd chosen Jo over her, she felt far less desirable right now. More like something he needed to scrape off his shiny black shoe.

Except his shoes weren't very shiny any more, after storming over the paddock. The ends of his pinstriped trousers looked a little worse for wear, too. No doubt he would blame Alice when he noticed and then she would have to face him again at work in the morning. Not that she had to do anything to gain this man's displeasure. Existing was more than enough.

Alice had to fight the urge to burst into tears the way Emmy had on hearing her father shouting. Just as well she was good at fighting. She'd learned to tap into stronger feelings. Like anger. She raised her chin.

'You might like to let Emmy's mother know it's not a good idea to let her wander around by herself,' she said crisply. 'The river's quite deep in places and it's not fenced off.'

Emmy turned again. She was shaking her head. 'I haven't got a mother,' she told Alice. 'She's dead, isn't she, Daddy?'

'Yes.' The monosyllabic response was giving nothing away.

It certainly wasn't inviting even one of the questions Alice had tumbling in her head. What had happened to Melissa? How long ago? Did Emmy miss her dreadfully? Did Andrew? Was that why he had decided to come to the other side of the world to be a solo parent?

'I've got a nanny instead,' Emmy continued.

'Not any more.' Andrew sounded weary now. 'Haylee's not going to be staying with us any longer.'

'Because she was so tired?'

That got a smile. One that Alice was completely excluded from. The bond between this father and daughter was clearly strong enough for her to have been forgotten as the two of them talked to each other. That impression was deepened as Andrew bent down and Emmy raised her arms to be picked up. And when she was, she wrapped her arms around her father's neck and her legs around his waist and tucked her head against his neck. A fluid series of movements that spoke of a well-rehearsed routine.

'Yes, sweetheart. Because she was too tired to look after you properly. Now say goodbye to Alice. We're going home.'

Emmy peeped over the solid wall of her father's shoulder. Big blue eyes and golden curls, just like her mother had had. The same kind of fragile prettiness that most men had found irresistible, but it had been Andrew that Mel had chosen.

'Goodbye, Alice,' the little girl said.

'Bye, hon.'

She was used to living here alone. It was more than five months since Mandy had gone. She had Ben. And Jake.

So why on earth did watching the retreating figure of Andrew, holding his child in his arms, make her feel not only alone but lonely?

Afraid, even.

CHAPTER THREE

'ARE you sure?'

'I'm sorry, Dr Barrett. This is a witnessed signature and all perfectly legal. The reason I wasn't aware of the sub-lease was because I was overseas at the time it was arranged and my junior partner dealt with it. Unfortunately, the filing of the document was incorrect.'

'So I'm stuck with it.'

'Only for another three weeks or thereabouts.' The solicitor raised an eyebrow. 'You didn't seem concerned about waiting for the lease to expire when you purchased the property.'

'That's because I had no idea who was really living in that cottage.'

'And the tenant is a problem?'

'Yes.' The word was heartfelt.

'In that case...' The solicitor smiled, pulling a blank piece of paper in front of him. 'What is she doing that's unacceptable?'

Andrew frowned. She was just...*there*; wasn't that enough? It was more than enough for him to find it disturbing. Especially when his daughter seemed convinced that Alice Palmer had magic powers of some kind. It was all she could talk about last night and she'd been almost breathless with excitement and talking so fast at times it had been hard to hear everything.

Apparently she had watched her gallop up a big hill with her hair streaming out behind.

'Like a real princess, Daddy. Will my hair grow that long one day?'

His precious daughter had been sitting on that monster of a horse that seemed to have a peculiar name, like Clock.

'Alice would teach me to ride if I asked really, really nicely, wouldn't she? She's a nice lady, isn't she, Daddy?'

The name of Ben had come up more than once in that non-stop stream of chatter that had carried on through dinner and bath time. It had even interrupted the bedtime story.

Andrew's nod was unconscious. 'She may be sharing the cottage,' he informed the solicitor, 'with a man by the name of Ben.'

'Ah…I'll have to check, Dr Barrett, but I'm not sure that would constitute breaking the terms of the lease agreement. Unfair eviction could lead to an appearance in the small claims court if this Ms Palmer was unduly upset by it. Is she—or this male companion—causing any damage to your property?'

'Not that I'm aware of.'

In fact, the neat flower beds and patch of vegetables he'd noticed as he carried Emmy past yesterday had made the area around the cottage look far better maintained than anything else on his vast new property. The general neglect had been something of a shock, to be honest, but that was the downside of making such a purchase via the Internet.

Andrew breathed out in a sigh. He didn't want to 'upset' Alice. Or find himself the bad guy in a minor court case. He would just have to grit his teeth and get through the next three weeks. And hope that Emmy didn't fall any further in love with this 'princess' she'd discovered.

He glanced at his watch. 'Never mind,' he growled. 'I don't have the time for this. I'm late enough for work as it is.'

At least the crisis involving Emmy's care had been temporarily solved. The school had an excellent care facility that was open for extended hours on either side of the school day. Peter had been very understanding about why Andrew would be late in today and he'd also promised to look at the shift roster later so that both the Barretts could get past this hiccup in the settling in process.

And that was all this was. A hiccup. One that might last a little longer than Andrew was happy with, but he could cope. He was still in control, after all.

'This sounds *perfect*!'

'What is it?'

'Five-acre property set up for the horse-lover. Three-bedroomed house, stables. There's a dressage arena and swimming pool and it's only thirty minutes drive to the CBD. Available immediately, it says.'

'How much?'

'Um...six hundred dollars a week.'

Alice almost choked on her coffee. 'Get real, Jo!'

'OK…' Jo scanned the newspaper column. 'How 'bout this? Two-bedroomed cottage on farm. Private and peaceful. Paddock available if required. Two hundred dollars a week.'

'Sounds promising.'

'Oh …' Jo groaned. 'It's way up in north Canterbury. Probably be a two-hour drive to work.'

A distinctly glum silence fell in the emergency department staff room.

'Do you really think you'll have to move?'

'Yeah…' Alice had no trouble recalling that expression on Andrew's face when he'd seen her on his property. 'And I've only got three weeks until my lease runs out. I might *have* to live in the wilds of north Canterbury.'

'It would certainly be peaceful,' Jo said wryly. 'Seriously, though. Couldn't you just find a paddock for Ben? Look, there's a whole section of grazing for hire. You could move in with me, then, while you're hunting.'

'Are you allowed dogs in your apartment? Large and particularly hairy ones?'

Jo shook her head sadly. 'Not even little bald ones. You wouldn't think of putting Jake in kennels? Just temporarily?'

'No way. He was an abandoned dog when I rescued him. I couldn't let him think it might be happening all over again.'

Jo sighed but smiled at the same time. 'You really love those critters of yours, don't you?'

'They're my family,' Alice said simply. 'No. There's got to be a way round this and I'm going to find it. Later…' She stood up abruptly. 'Come on, Jo. We're short-staffed and we were only supposed to be having a two-minute break, remember?'

'We're not *that* busy.'

'Don't even think like that. You're tempting fate.'

Andrew pushed open the double doors of the emergency department, having left his suit jacket and briefcase in his office, and paused, taking in what appeared to be a scene of bedlam.

The curtains on all three resuscitation areas were pulled shut and the sound of screaming was coming from somewhere behind them. Technicians and nurses were going in all directions. One was pushing a trolley into Resus 1. Another came from Resus 2 with a sealed bag of blood samples and she was heading for the vacuum tube system that would suck them straight to the laboratory. An orderly was trying to manoeuvre a bed past two ambulance stretchers queuing for the attention of the triage nurse. The cubicles all looked occupied.

So early in the day and it was chaos. Controlled, but only just.

Cursing the fact that he was well over an hour late to start his shift, Andrew made a beeline for the triage nurse, trying to ignore the fact that the person doing this important job today was the one person he least wanted to see.

Alice was talking to one of the paramedics standing beside the first stretcher.

'I'm afraid a sprained ankle isn't going to get a high priority at the moment. Can you find a wheelchair and take her through to Reception?' She glanced up and spotted Andrew's approach.

A flicker of something like fear washed across her features, which gave Andrew a pang of something rather like shame. He repressed it firmly. This was good. He was in control and Alice Palmer knew it.

'What's going on?' he queried crisply. 'And where am I needed?'

'We've got major trauma from an MVA in Resus 1 and 2,' Alice told him in exactly the same tone. 'We need someone circulating for the moment.'

Circulating? Looking at minor cases in the cubicles when there was major trauma to deal with? Alice might have the responsibility of assigning priority to patients and deploying the department's resources, but this felt remarkably like her trying to undermine his control.

'Where are all the junior staff?'

'One's gone to CT with an unstable stroke patient. I've got two in the middle of dealing with an arterial laceration and the rest are tied up with the trauma cases. There's a cardiac chest pain in Resus 3 that hasn't been assessed yet.'

'Peter?'

'Resus 1.'

More staff were arriving. Specialists summoned to help deal with the car accident victims. Andrew recognised a cardio-thoracic surgeon and an anaesthetist pushing through the curtains of the first Resus area. In the gap they created, he could see the huge team of departmental staff surrounding the bed in there. They didn't need another consultant.

An alarm sounded from an overhead monitor and Alice glanced up swiftly, touching a button to silence the alarm.

'Resus 3,' she said calmly. 'VPBs.'

Her gaze caught Andrew's and he nodded. The cardiac patient was unstable and his rhythm suggested that he could deteriorate at any time. Even as the thought formulated, the alarm sounded again.

'VF. I'll get the crash cart.' Alice was already moving, turning her head only briefly to look towards the cubicle area. 'Jo? Take over triage, would you, please?'

They arrived in the third Resus area at the same time but it was Alice who took the lead. She had the head of the bed flattened in less time than it took Andrew to step towards the bed. Then she raised her fist and thumped the middle-aged man in the centre of his chest.

A precordial thump. Sometimes, it was enough to jerk the heart into producing a viable rhythm again. Not this time. Andrew tilted the man's head back to open his airway, pulling off the oxygen mask. He found a bag-mask being handed to him. How had Alice managed that at the same time as sticking the gel pads to the man's chest?

'Shock?' she queried succinctly.

'You do it,' Andrew said. 'Where's the airway trolley?'

'Right behind you. Stand clear.' Alice had her finger poised over the button on the defibrillator as the sound of the machine gathering its charge changed to an alarm.

'I'm clear.' Andrew unrolled a sterile cloth that contained everything he would need to intubate the patient if necessary.

'Shocking again at 360,' Alice said. 'Clear.'

'I'm clear.'

A third stacked shock was delivered but there was no

change to the fatal rhythm showing on the monitor. Andrew delivered another lungful of air with the bag mask, noting Alice's perfect hand position as she started chest compressions.

'Where's the rest of the crash crew?'

'Obviously busy.' Alice kept pressing, one hand on top of the other. The sound of agonised groaning was coming from behind the curtain. He could also hear machinery being manoeuvred and orders being barked with the kind of urgency that advertised a struggle to save a life.

'Twenty-five, twenty-six, twenty-seven...' Alice counted aloud.

Andrew picked up the bag-mask again. He would be due to deliver another two breaths when she got to thirty.

'I need someone else in here,' he snapped.

Alice paused to let him deliver the oxygen. 'This is where I work, Andrew.' She might be slightly breathless but the tone was final enough. 'Deal with it.'

It took the blink of an eye for Andrew to realise she'd misunderstood. '*We* need someone else in here,' he said tightly. For goodness' sake, how inappropriate was it to bring personal issues to this kind of scene? 'I need IV access. Some adrenaline drawn up. I'll want some assistance to intubate and I want uninterrupted CPR.'

Alice looked up. Her gaze was determined. Confident. 'If we have to,' she said calmly, 'we'll manage.'

And, somehow, they did.

Extra staff arrived five minutes later but they could only stand and watch. Their patient's airway was secure. IV drugs had been administered and...best of all...a viable rhythm was showing on the monitor.

'Good save,' someone said.

Alice was still on the other side of the unconscious man. She had her fingers on the man's wrist, checking the strength of his radial pulse. Again, she looked up and caught Andrew's gaze and, this time, she held it for a fraction longer.

There was satisfaction in her eyes. Triumph, even. And more. Andrew could see the warm acknowledgement that this had been a team effort. Neither of them could have managed this without the other.

Her face was flushed from the stress and the effort of doing CPR. Some tiny curls had escaped the tight braid her hair was tied back in and one was stuck on her cheek. The dusting of freckles on her nose was like a faint splash of colour coming from the deep auburn of that wayward curl. And her eyes! Was it the triumph of a job well done that made those golden flecks shine against a background of dark hazel? Or were they catching the glow from lips that were lifting into a smile?

'We did it,' Alice said. 'Well done us.'

Andrew could only nod. Returning the smile was too much of an ask when he was grappling with the horrible awareness that he found this woman attractive.

Very attractive.

As if she wasn't causing enough of a problem in his life already, here he was, fighting a ridiculous urge to lean across and brush that curl back into place.

A movement from their patient mercifully doused the disturbing thought.

'He's lightening up.'

'Spontaneous respiration,' Alice noted.

Andrew considered sedation but the rhythm on the screen was steady now. Looking remarkably normal, in fact.

'Let's get that tube out,' he decided. 'And get the cardiologists to come and sort this chap out.'

With a bit of luck, he would be able to sort his own problems concerning Alice Palmer out with equal success. The fact that she was an undeniably attractive woman made no difference.

None at all.

So why did he seem to become increasingly aware of her as the day wore on? He noticed her deftly slipping an IV cannula into a patient's arm as he walked past a cubicle. Saw her patiently supporting a very elderly woman as they moved very slowly towards the toilets. Got caught in the backwash of the smile she sent her friend, Jo, as they passed each other pushing wheelchairs.

It simply wouldn't do.

Fortunately, the department became a lot quieter in the afternoon.

'You needed to get away early, didn't you?' Peter queried. 'To collect your daughter.'

'I should stay on. I still feel bad about being so late in this morning.'

Peter smiled as he shook his head. 'Hardly your fault the place was chaos. You did well managing that arrest on your own.'

'I wasn't entirely on my own.'

'No.' The head of department seemed to be giving him a curiously intent glance. 'Alice is worth her weight in gold, isn't she?'

Gold. Like those flecks in her eyes.

'Indeed.' Andrew's tone was far more level than his state of mind in that instant.

His heart was sinking rapidly on two fronts. Not only had he failed to squash this unwanted awareness of Alice's appearance but his boss seemed to be giving him a subtle warning that she was a valued staff member. Had he picked up vibes that they were finding it difficult to work together?

Had Alice said something to him?

She happened to be behind the triage desk again, only a few steps from where Peter had paused to speak to Andrew and suggest he head home. He could have sworn she sensed his gaze when she looked up and her expression was slightly startled. A flush of colour touched her cheeks—as though she was also aware of his suspicion. As if his suspicion was justified.

Andrew took those few steps towards the desk as soon as his brief conversation with Peter was finished.

Alice threw a swift glance over her shoulder but there was no one within earshot. She raised her chin and met Andrew's gaze squarely.

'You have a problem?'

'I think we might both have a problem,' Andrew said very quietly. 'Don't you?'

'I know I do,' Alice retorted softly. 'Being evicted from my home could certainly be considered a problem.'

'The lease is due to expire. Renewing it is simply not an option.'

The upward quirk of her eyebrows suggested otherwise.

'I need help with my property,' Andrew said evenly,

'and responsible care for my daughter. I don't want staff living in my house and that makes the cottage you're inhabiting essential for other purposes. It's not personal,' he added.

This time the eyebrows were joined by a wry twist of her mouth. 'Sure.'

Andrew sighed. 'Did you really think I was stating a personal preference when I said I needed someone else in that arrest scenario?'

Alice looked away. She focused on one of the telephones on the desk in front of her as though she expected it to ring. Or wanted it to.

'You've made it obvious that you aren't exactly thrilled to be working with me,' she said finally. 'You still believe I took those drugs, don't you?'

'I never said that.' The words came out more fiercely than intended. 'Did I?'

She was silent for a long moment. When she spoke again, her voice was so low that Andrew had to duck his head to catch the words.

'You said you couldn't trust me.'

He had said that. As a departmental head with the responsibilities of many others to consider it was the stance he'd been forced to adopt. He couldn't have afforded to trust her at that point in time, no matter what his heart might have told him.

And maybe he still couldn't. He wanted to, but she had the power to undermine his desperate wish to start again. To build a new life. Something that was too precious to risk.

Alice had looked up again. There was a challenge in her face. And...and *hope*, dammit! This was his chance to undo the wrong he had done. He could restore a pride that she had every right to have in herself. All he had to do was deny his mistrust.

He opened his mouth to do exactly that but there was a heartbeat's worth of hesitation before any sound emerged. Just long enough to recognise that yes, the mistrust was still there, but it was personal and not professional and he could therefore answer her with conviction.

But the damage had been done in that tiny fraction of time. He saw the way that hope died in her eyes. The way she turned away, holding up her hand to stop him saying anything.

'Don't bother,' she snapped. 'I really don't want to hear it.' Her back straightened noticeably. 'We both work here and we'll both have to deal with it. Let's keep it professional, shall we, and leave anything personal in the past.'

That suited Andrew admirably. 'Sure.'

'If you have any issues with my performance as a nurse in this department, feel free to discuss them with me. Or you can refer them directly to Peter.'

'I don't expect to have any issues.'

'Good.' Alice was reaching for the phone that was now ringing. 'Neither do I.'

Had she really expected him to pat her on the back and say that of course he didn't believe she had stolen restricted drugs? That he trusted her? Why had she even entertained such a hope? Because they had worked so well together on that arrest case? He was good at his job. So was she. Being able to work as a competent team should have nothing to do with how they felt about each other on a personal level.

She was the one who'd been unprofessional and made it personal. Extra staff were certainly called for to deal with a cardiac arrest but she'd misunderstood. Not only that, she'd attacked as a form of defence. Remembering her tone of voice was enough to make Alice cringe even now, when she'd been at home for long enough to exercise and feed her pets and unwind from her day. Had she sealed her own fate by remind-ing Andrew of the past like that? Especially then?

The scene had not been dissimilar to what had hap-pened just prior to the final straw regarding her employ-ment under Andrew's watch. There'd been a big pile-up on the motorway and Emergency had been stretched to the limits of everyone's abilities. The cardiac arrest had had no chance of being successfully managed when it had been due to such major chest injuries, but she'd been the one working alongside Andrew.

Just how that ampoule of morphine had got into the pocket of her tunic was still a mystery. Or why Andrew had chosen that day to ask her to empty her pockets. On top of the history of drugs going missing on her shifts and the empty ampoules found in her locker, it had spelt the end. Maybe someone else could have planted the empty ampoules, but why would they have put one in Alice's pocket that day? The weight of evidence had been too heavy, despite tearful denial on her part.

Right now, when she was at home and in a place that had always put anything negative into perspective, Alice had the horrible sensation that a ticking clock had replaced her heartbeat for the purpose of reminding her that this refuge was temporary. That any hope of remaining here was in the hands of a man she had just reminded why he couldn't bring himself to trust her.

Positive thinking could only go so far to counteract feeling powerless.

Vulnerable.

It wasn't nearly far enough.

Alice went through her usual routine, but her actions were so mechanical she forgot the little extras like having music on while she cooked the dinner or lighting a scented candle to enjoy while having her bath. She even forgot the cup of tea she always made when she turned on the computer to check her email before going to bed.

The message from her old friend in London was a welcome surprise in her inbox. A bit of moral support from someone who would understand was exactly what she needed. Alice double-clicked to bring the email to full screen size.

'Good to hear from you at long last,' Pam had written. And then, after expressing sympathy for the process of finally dealing with her grandmother's estate. *'I'm gobsmacked to hear that Randy Andy has turned up in your neck of the woods!'*

The nickname grated. It always had. Sure, Andrew had had a reputation with women, but it hadn't taken long for Alice to realise that it was the women who did the running and that they never got as far as they wanted with the eligible young doctor. Except for Melissa, of course—the vivacious blonde who'd been assigned to showing Alice the ropes in her new job.

'Forget it,' she'd smiled, after introducing the newcomer to the head of department. 'He's mine.'

'He is,' Pam had confirmed as her friendship with Alice blossomed. 'Or he will be. You just watch.'

Alice *had* watched with disbelief that a man as intelligent as Andrew could have fallen for the campaign. Could he not see that Melissa was more interested in him as a status symbol and guarantee of a secure future? Surely he would see through it. And then he'd see that another woman might be able to offer something a lot more meaningful.

It had been hard to give up the wish that she could be that other woman. Even when Andrew had done absolutely nothing to suggest he would be anything other than faithful to the woman he was in a relationship with. She'd been invited to the wedding six months later, where Melissa's smile had only hinted at triumph and the gorgeous dress made sure that no signs of her pregnancy were showing.

'Mind you,' Pam's email continued, *'I'm not surprised that he went as far away as possible. I was with you on those rumours after Mel kept turning up with those injuries like the broken wrist and the bruises but now I just don't know what to think. It added up to a pretty nasty picture when the file got pulled in for that last admission.'*

So Pam had been there. Alice's lips were parted as she leaned forward a little, reading on swiftly. The gap between her lips grew wider as the unfolding story made her jaw drop.

'She'd fallen down this set of concrete steps,' Pam reported. *'Awful head injuries. She got taken to Theatre but never regained consciousness. She was in ICU on*

a ventilator for weeks and it was all anyone could talk about. The police were involved and what with the evidence in her file right from the start of that marriage there were noises about charges being laid. One of the porters overheard a cop saying that there was a suggestion that Mel had been pushed rather than fallen down those steps.'

Alice's breath came out in a gasp.

No!

She hadn't only watched Melissa in action stalking her intended husband over those months. She'd watched Andrew as well. Had worked with him. Had seen and heard enough to know exactly why Melissa and so many others thought of him as a prize. It wasn't just his looks, though, heaven knew, they were enough. The man was an exceptionally talented doctor without being arrogant about it. He had been generous with his time and knowledge.

And he was gentle. The quality that had captured Alice more than any other. She had seen him use split second initiative, skill and strength to do something like cracking a chest or relocating a dislocated shoulder, but she'd also seen him take the time to do procedures as painlessly as possible. Even if he was over-committed and especially if the patient was a child. She'd seen him reassure a frightened person with words or a touch or...that smile. The one that made the lines deepen around those incredibly blue eyes. That made his face soften and change so you just *knew* how absolutely sincere it was. The smile that had made Alice realise she had—unintentionally—fallen in love with him herself.

She hadn't seen quite that smile since his reappearance in her life but she'd seen that his manner with patients hadn't changed. She'd seen the bond he had with his daughter. There was simply no way she could ever believe he had deliberately pushed his wife down a set of steps. It was…outrageous.

'I never heard what happened in the end,' Pam's account continued. *'Andy got suspended as soon as the police investigation got underway and then it just fizzled out. The coroner's report was accidental death and no charges ever got laid but he never came back to work.'*

Why would he? Alice knew better than anyone what it was like to be suspected of something you hadn't done. How impossible it could be to prove innocence and completely clear your name. How the taint of suspicion poisoned everything.

She'd come all the way back to New Zealand to start again, but Andrew's move was braver because he was coming somewhere he'd never been before. As a single father with a young child and no support network of friends and family to help. Alice knew why. He wouldn't want to live with that poison. Imagine if Emmy grew up to hear rumours that her father might have somehow contributed to the death of her mother.

It would be worse than an allegation of stealing drugs, wouldn't it?

Alice sat back, the rest of Pam's chatty email, about the new HoD and who was dating whom, turning into a blur.

Andrew Barrett had more to lose than she did. Someone who knew his history was a threat that could affect his entire life—professional and personal.

A huff of something like laughter escaped her lips. Not only had the poor guy found her working in his new department, he'd come to his new home and found her living on the property.

Unfair.

Ironic.

And, despite the worry about her own situation and the hurt that Andrew's lack of trust still generated, Alice's overriding reaction was to want to reach out to him.

To comfort him.

To tell him that she didn't believe any of it.

She had to try and curb the impulse. Giving him any indication that she cared about him or his daughter to that extent would only make herself more vulnerable. And why should she step out on that limb when Andrew wasn't even prepared to give *her* the benefit of any doubt?

It was impossible to squash her reaction completely, however, and maybe that was a good thing. Alice was too shocked to be able to think clearly right now but surely, if Andrew knew that there was someone on his side—a *friend*—it couldn't hurt, could it? It might even make him reconsider his decision about her lease.

'Things happen for a reason,' she told Jake, as he slumped to the floor beside her bed. Alice flicked off the light and stared up at the ceiling. 'This might sound crazy but there's a remote possibility that all this could turn out to be the best thing that's ever happened to me.'

CHAPTER FOUR

'GOOD morning, Dr Barrett.'

'Ah…good morning, Alice.'

Her cheerful smile had clearly unsettled Andrew. He wasn't expecting her to be happy to see him arrive for work. In fact, the sideways glance he sent her, before checking the pile of notes that had just been delivered to the central desk area, had a distinctly suspicious tinge.

But Alice *was* feeling cheerful. Confident, even. So much better than she'd been feeling yesterday, before receiving that astonishing email from Pam. Being friendly was the safest and easiest course to follow for the moment and it might even work. She knew that Andrew was a good man. He wouldn't set out to make life unbearable for anyone and he would probably do a great deal to help a friend.

'Glorious sunrise this morning, wasn't it?' She'd driven into it on her way to a 7:00 a.m. start. Andrew would have been in a much better position to admire the silhouette of craggy hills against the amazing red glow.

'Mmm.' He'd selected a set of notes. He looked up

at the white board to find the location of the patient he
was intending to see.

'April's the best month in Canterbury.' For some reason, Alice couldn't let it go at such a brief, professional
kind of exchange. 'Bit of a nip in the mornings but then
we get these lovely sunny, still days.'

She was looking at the back of Andrew's head, wondering if he would continue to ignore her. It was quite
unfair for a man to have natural streaks of gold that so
many women were prepared to pay a fortune to have a
hairdresser emulate. He must have been quite blond as
a child. Maybe that was where Emmy got the genes
from, because, if her memory served her correctly, it
hadn't been the shade Melissa had been born with.

'Cold at night, though.' Carrying on this one-sided
conversation was a kind of disguise for what she was
really thinking about. Alice made it seem even more
casual by turning back to her own task of searching for a
GP's referral letter that had been faxed through prior to a
patient's arrival. 'You must be noticing it in that big
house.'

'Not really.' Andrew made it sound a strain to be
polite. 'I'm having the chimneys swept today and a
load of firewood being delivered.'

'But you've got any amount of firewood for free!
There's dozens of dead tree branches all over the place.
All you need is a chainsaw.'

'Good point.' Andrew's smile was tight. 'Thanks for
the tip. I'll put it on the list of equipment I need.'

He was moving away now, the notes clutched in one
hand. Alice couldn't help the sudden vision of a chainsaw hanging there instead. Of Andrew transformed into

a good Kiwi bloke, wearing ripped old blue jeans and a black singlet. With the muscles in his shoulders rippling as he pulled the cord to start the motor of the heavy tool.

Her mouth felt curiously dry all of a sudden.

'Pine cones,' she heard herself say in a kind of croak.

Andrew turned his head. 'Sorry?'

'You'll want pine cones.' Her voice sounded more normal now. She could even add a friendly smile. 'Best thing to start fires with. That stand of trees where I park the horse float has heaps of them. Emmy would enjoy collecting them.'

Andrew said nothing. His face suggested that she had no business suggesting what his daughter might enjoy doing. Or giving him advice about power tools or how to start fires. It was just as well he had no idea of the way her stomach had done that peculiar little flip, imagining him with that particular power tool.

Confidence was one thing. Stepping into a space where she was aware of Andrew Barrett's personal attributes was something entirely different.

Don't do it, Alice warned herself sternly. *Don't even think of going there again.*

It would be nothing less than self-sabotage. The notion of a relationship within the safe boundaries of friendship was giving her a way forward. Confidence. Hope that she could keep what she really wanted, which was to keep living exactly where she was. Contemplating making herself vulnerable all over again by going back to finding this man irresistibly attractive was simply not an option.

Peter saved her from having to dwell on such a disturbing option.

'We're short in the observation area, Alice. You wouldn't fancy a stint in there today, would you?'

'Sure.' It wasn't normally her favourite place to work, being well away from the acute management or resuscitation of major cases that came in, but, right now, it was perfect. It would also be well away from their newest consultant.

Except it wasn't.

Eight-year-old Luke had responded well to the management of his asthma when he'd been brought in by ambulance shortly after Alice had started her shift. He'd been resting quietly in one of the cubicles in the observation area ever since but his condition was deteriorating again. Alice could hear the increase in the wheezing sound he was making as she walked past the end of his bed. When she went closer, it was all too easy to see his small ribs protruding with the effort the boy was making to breathe.

'Has Mum gone to get your little sister from kindergarten?'

Luke nodded. His eyes were suspiciously bright and Alice wondered if he'd been more upset than he'd let on at being temporarily abandoned by his mother. Something had certainly triggered his asthma again.

'I'm going to put some more Salbutamol in your nebuliser,' she told him. 'And we'll put this clip back on your finger.' She attached the oxygen saturation monitor. 'And now I'm going to get your doctor to come and check you again.'

The doctor who'd seen Luke early this morning had been off duty for hours. The doctor that came in response to her message to the front desk was Andrew.

'Hey, Luke. How's it going, buddy?' He picked up the chart from the end of Luke's bed.

'Initial attack was moderate to mild,' Alice informed him quietly. 'Pulse ox ninety-four per cent. He responded well to nebulised Salbutamol.'

He wasn't responding well now. Luke's heart and respiration rates were soaring and the oxygen level in his blood was dropping steadily. The little boy was looking tired as well and fatigue could be a major contributing factor to a respiratory arrest which could turn this asthma attack into a life-threatening emergency within minutes.

'Let's add some Ipratropium to that nebuliser,' Andrew said calmly. He perched on the bed with one hip as he picked up Luke's hand. 'You're doing great,' he told the boy. His thumb rubbed over the plaster on the small hand and Andrew raised an eyebrow at Alice. 'IV access?'

'It wasn't used and tissued an hour or so ago. The paediatric registrar said it was okay to remove.'

The tiny frown was a sympathetic flicker and Alice could see the small hand being given a squeeze. 'Luke?' Andrew's tone was gentle. 'I need to pop another wee needle in your arm.'

'No-ooo!' The word was a gasp.

'Sorry, buddy, but we need to give you some more medicine to help your breathing.'

Alice stepped closer, lifting the nebuliser mask to add the requested new drug to the attached chamber. She also squeezed in a new ampoule of Salbutamol and then she eased the mask back over Luke's face and gave his hair a ruffle.

'Dr Barrett is really, really good at this,' she told Luke. 'Better than anybody.'

She gave the boy's shoulder a reassuring squeeze as the tourniquet was snapped into place, noting the way Andrew kept all the other supplies he needed out of sight. All he showed Luke was a small can.

'This stuff is fantastic,' he said. 'It's like spray ice so it stops things hurting too much.' He sprayed the back of Luke's hand.

And then he seemed to forget what he was doing. He stared at one of the bright posters decorating this cubicle that was kept for paediatric cases. 'Look at that poster over there,' he said, sounding astonished. 'Is that elephant really doing what I *think* he's doing?'

The elephant in the picture wasn't doing anything extraordinary, but by the time Luke had looked at the wall and then back again, the cannula was in his vein.

Andrew smiled. 'All done. Wasn't so bad, was it?'

Luke shook his head, too breathless to speak.

Alice felt rather breathless herself. It had been one of *those* smiles. The crinkly-eyed, glowing kind. And it touched a spot on her heart that she had been so sure had healed over completely. It was bad enough being aware of how attractive Andrew was again. It was far, far worse to recognise the kind of connection that only came from being in love with someone.

She held Luke's arm steady to avoid any sudden jerks that might dislodge the cannula, watching as Andrew taped it into place, aware of a growing sense of dismay.

So it was still there. In spades. That awareness of how deft his movements were. How familiar the sight of those hands was because she'd watched them too often in the past. She knew about that tiny scar on his forefinger and how neatly cut his nails always were. She also knew, only too well, what it was like to imagine those fingers touching her own skin. This was no glow from stirred up ashes. Flames were flickering as though they'd never been doused.

'I want some oral Prednisolone,' Andrew was saying as he looked up.

And then he blinked, stopping for just a heartbeat with his lips still parted, and Alice had the truly horrible thought that he could see into her head.

Into her heart.

'Two milligrams per kilogram.' Andrew cleared his throat. 'Get some hydrocortisone drawn up as backup, too, please. Keep up the continuous nebulised Salbutamol and I'd like some IV Salbutamol drawn up as well. I'm going to give Paeds a quick call.'

Alice nodded briskly. This was good. She had plenty to do and a patient to focus on. Andrew would forget about whatever fleeting impression he'd got from her expression and she would make sure he didn't get so much as a sniff of anything less than purely professional interaction from now on.

She knew the worst. She was prepared. If possible, she would avoid any interaction at all. She might even revisit the idea of working in another department for a while. It was probably just the surprise of having this man in her life again that was triggering such an unwelcome reaction. She would get over it. Again.

Luke's asthma attack came under control with satisfying speed but he was admitted to the paediatric ward for close monitoring. For the rest of her shift, Alice put her hand up for every task that took her away from the department. Accompanying patients to specialist test areas, sitting in with social workers making an assessment, even taking on some sluice room duties everyone else was avoiding.

The strategy worked. She didn't even see Andrew again until she was ready to leave at three p.m. She would have avoided him then, too, as she walked down the corridor to the outside doors, but he stepped right into her path.

'Have you got a minute, Alice?'

'Not really. I'm heading home.'

'You're keen to get away, then?'

'You bet. It's a gorgeous day and I want to get home in time to ride Ben before it's dark.'

Andrew had the oddest expression on his face by the time she had finished speaking. He seemed to shrink away from her.

'Ben?'

Alice nodded slowly. 'My horse. You met him, remember? The monster?'

Andrew gave his head a tiny shake, as though trying to clear it. 'Emmy said your horse was called Clock.'

Alice grinned. 'He's Big Ben. Named *after* the clock.'

'Ohh…'

A smile was tugging at the corners of Andrew's mouth but didn't quite succeed. He looked as if he was trying hard not to look pleased. Alice mentally played back the snippet of conversation they'd just had and found herself staring even more intently than she had been. He'd been pleased to discover Ben was a horse.

Why?

The warmth that flickered into life deep inside Alice told her it was because he was feeling some degree of the attraction she was struggling with. If he was, however, it had to be purely a physical reaction. He didn't trust her so it was a no-brainer that it could never be anything more.

Which made it far more dangerous for her because, at the end of the day, if she allowed herself to care again she stood to lose far more than Andrew did.

And that was way too much.

Emmy sat inside the big orange wheelbarrow, gripping each side and bouncing as Andrew propelled it forward over the uneven ground.

'Go faster, Daddy!'

'No. You might fall out.'

'I won't!'

'You might. Besides, we're here already. Look at all these pine cones just waiting for us to pick up.'

'Oooh!' Emmy was climbing out of the wheelbarrow even before it came to a complete halt. 'Are we going to have a fire?'

'We sure are. We bought marshmallows on the way home, remember?'

'I like the pink ones.' Emmy picked up one large pine cone and held it between both hands. She walked importantly back to the barrow and dropped her prize with a flourish.

Andrew hid his grin, swooping to pick up two cones in each hand. This wouldn't take long, despite Emmy's efforts being so laboured, and that was just as well because it was nearly 6:00 p.m. and daylight was fading fast. The chimneys had been swept and the huge mound of split firewood waiting to be stacked was nice and dry. With the help of the cones, he would have a roaring fire going to ward off the chill of the autumn evening before he turned his attention to preparing their dinner.

Dropping another armload of cones into the barrow, Andrew straightened, taking a moment to soak in the sight of Emmy's golden head shining against the dark backdrop of tree trunks. She was squatting and poking at the ground with a stick, clearly absorbed with a new discovery, the task of collecting kindling forgotten. It didn't matter. This kind of time with his daughter and the new adventures waiting for them both were exactly why he'd come here. Emmy was loving it.

Just as Alice had suggested she would.

Thinking about Alice was an unwelcome intrusion but it was hard not to when her horse float was parked not far from where he stood. Turning his head, Andrew could see the cottage. He could see Alice, in fact, hanging some washing on a line strung between two trees.

'Em?'

'I found a bug, Daddy. A big, shiny black one.'

'Can you find some more pine cones? We need to get a move on.'

'Soon.'

'Do it now, sweetheart, or we might not be able to toast marshmallows for supper.'

'Oh. Okay.' Emmy jumped up and ran towards him with a cone. 'Oooh, look, Daddy! There's Alice!'

'So it is.'

'Can I go and ask if I can pat the horse?'

'Not today.'

'When?'

'Alice is busy. See? She's hanging out her washing.'

'You could ask her, Daddy. Ask her when she won't be too busy and when I could have another ride. She said I could if you said I could. Please, Daddy. Please?'

The small face was turned up to his and the desperate desire he could see written all over it was irresistible.

'I'll ask.'

'Now?'

'Not now. We're busy collecting our pine cones.'

'I'll get lots of cones. You go and talk to Alice.' Emmy took a huge breath and held it. *'Please?'*

Andrew sighed. 'Okay. But don't you go anywhere. See how many cones you can find.'

'Sorry to disturb you.'

Oh…God! It was bad enough to have her unwilling landlord turn up in her back garden when she was wearing her dirty jodhpurs and ancient gumboots and a tattered old woollen jersey, but why did he have to pick the precise moment she was pegging out her underwear? At least it was her best pair of knickers—the silky ones that had a nice bit of lace at the top.

He was staring at the small item of clothing and, to his credit, he looked discomfited when he recognised what it was.

'Ah …' Andrew cleared his throat and looked away, but his gaze raked hers on the way and Alice had the impression that he'd been imagining her wearing those knickers.

'I'm almost done.' Alice dived for the last item in her basket. Dammit! It was the bra that matched those knickers. Andrew was looking into the basket as well now. If she just left the bra there, he'd know she was embarrassed and he might guess that the reason for that embarrassment was her awareness of him. Her resolve to keep that awareness totally hidden had to be found and acted on.

Easy, really, if you thought of it the same way as doing something you knew would be embarrassing for a patient. Alice simply had to be matter-of-fact. Brisk and competent. As though she was so used to doing this that it failed to register.

'I know it's a funny time of day to be hanging out washing,' she admitted breezily as she fished for a peg, 'but I leave for work at 6:00 a.m. and it's too dark in the mornings, now.'

'It is quite a drive into town. What made you want to live this far out?'

'You bought this place without setting foot on it, didn't you?'

'I sent an agent to check it out.'

'And that was enough?'

'The pictures were pretty compelling, I have to say.'

'Hmm.' Alice picked up the wooden pole with a deep groove in the top. She put the rope of the clothes line into the groove and then walked forward, straightening the pole and lifting the line high enough to clear the barrier it had made between herself and Andrew. 'That would have been enough to catch the magic,' she agreed. 'I came out to visit Mandy and fell in love.'

Oh, Lord! Why had she used that particular phrase?

Even if she wanted to convey how important it was for her to stay here, the words were inappropriate. Too personal. Possibly too revealing. Alice looked away in a quiet plea for distraction and there it was. She waved at Emmy. Jake left his position beside the tin that held the clothes pegs and moved towards the small figure, his tail waving in a friendly greeting.

'Looks like you're getting a good supply of pine cones.'

'Yes.' Andrew looked back at his daughter and frowned. 'Is that dog safe with children?'

'Absolutely.'

Andrew was still frowning. 'Emmy wanted me to come and talk to you. She's dead set on visiting your horse again.'

'Ben.'

'Yes…Ben.' Andrew wasn't meeting her gaze now and Alice found herself smiling inwardly. Maybe it was his turn to feel embarrassed. But then he did meet her eyes and any intention Alice had of keeping this brisk and impersonal went out the window. She couldn't look away and the contact went on just that bit too long. Long enough for questions to be formed on both sides. Questions she was determined not to ask that needed answers she was certainly not about to supply. She had to find a way of creating a safe distance here.

'You don't want her to.'

'Sorry?' Andrew appeared to have lost the thread of their conversation.

'You don't want Emmy visiting Ben.'

'No, I don't think I do.'

'Because you think he's dangerous? I can assure you he's not. He's the most—'

Andrew was shaking his head. 'That's not the reason.'

'What is?'

He took another quick glance over his shoulder and Alice followed his line of vision. The wheelbarrow was apparently full and Emmy was crouched beside it, her arms around Jake as she hugged the dog. It was dark enough to be harder to see the little girl now except that her hair shone like a halo.

Andrew turned back. 'As you can see, Emmy forms attachments easily. She adores animals and...' he seemed to be scowling at Alice now '...she seems to have taken a fancy to you. She thinks you're a princess in disguise or something.'

Alice smiled. 'She's a cute kid.'

The smile wasn't returned. Andrew looked away. 'The lease on this cottage expires in three weeks and you'll have to leave by then. Preferably sooner. I don't want Emmy upset by your departure and the closer she gets to you and your animals, the more likely that is to happen.'

He knew the names of her pets. It was a deliberate put-down to refer to them as simply 'animals'.

And he wanted her to be gone even before the lease had expired? Would it make any difference if he knew how impossible it was going to be to find somewhere affordable to go, never mind having to pack up her life and shift?

No. He wouldn't care, even if he did understand. Maybe Andrew Barrett came across as caring and gentle and wonderful with his patients, but, on a personal level, Alice had clearly made a big mistake in her opinion of him and, just as clearly, any kind of friendship was not going to be an option. She drew in a careful breath.

This was it. Her salvation. She had another opportunity to flip that coin and learn to hate this man, and if she could succeed this time, then she would have no problem finding the energy and strength she needed to deal with whatever came from any association she had with him. She would escape. Find somewhere else to live and another department to work in. Another *city* to work in, maybe, however painful it would be to up sticks and start all over again.

Some of that pain was already setting in and it made her want to lash out. In defence of her 'animals' if nothing else.

'I need longer than three weeks,' she said. 'It's not easy to find rental property that allows for keeping a horse and a dog.'

'Not my problem, I'm sorry.' Andrew seemed to be finding her gumboots of extraordinary interest. 'I've explained why I need this cottage. It's urgent that I get a suitable childcare arrangement in place. I was late for work yesterday and I can't expect new colleagues to keep picking up any slack.'

He finally looked up and the distance Alice could feel was far greater than when he'd first seen her in the emergency department. He was trying to get as far away as possible and he certainly wasn't going to give an inch as far as her problems were concerned.

This was hopeless. It seemed even more hopeless when Andrew turned his back on her. The conversation was over. Her life, as she currently knew and loved it, also appeared to be over.

'No, I don't suppose you can.' The words came from nowhere, filled with the pain of her own imminent loss. 'I don't suppose you want those new colleagues to know the details of why you've come here, either.'

He turned, very slowly. Even in this half light of dusk, Alice could see the way the colour left Andrew's face.

He didn't have to say a word. The awful allegations he'd had to face hung in the air between them. So did the fact that Alice knew about them. That she could make life very difficult for him if she chose to.

It should have been a triumphant moment, a shift in the balance of power, but instead Alice felt…mortified.

It was a horrible thing to have said. She wanted to pull the words back and she dragged in a new breath to do exactly that. To tell Andrew that she knew how absurd the suspicion had been. That she hadn't believed a single one of those rumours.

That it didn't matter if he evicted her or made work difficult, she would never start a new spread of poisonous gossip. In fact, she would defend him if someone else said anything.

Like she always had.

This was unbelievable.

History was repeating itself.

Blackmail. By a woman. God, did they all think like that? That it was morally acceptable to use whatever means it took to get what they wanted? He should have learned his lesson about trusting women by now.

'I'm pregnant, Andy. You have to marry me.'

'Stay with me or I won't even go near Rehab.'

'Keep quiet or I'll take your daughter away and you'll never see her again.'

Anger came from nowhere. A painfully intense shaft that made him clench a fist and raise it unconsciously as he tried to find the words he needed to tell Alice Palmer exactly what he thought of her and her threat.

He could see her taking in a breath. Opening her mouth to say something. Then he saw the expression on her face change and there was no mistaking the flash of fear.

Oh…*God*! Did she really think he might *hit* her?

His hand unclenched but still moved towards her. He needed to touch her. To apologise and wipe that fear from her eyes. But Alice wasn't looking at him now. Her head had swivelled and she took a step away from him.

'Jake?' she called. 'What's wrong?'

Andrew could hear it now. A volley of barks coming from some distance away. Urgent barking that wasn't stopping.

His own head moved as swiftly as Alice's had. Looking back at the trees and the wheelbarrow to where the dog had last been seen.

To where his daughter had been.

'Oh…*no*!' The word was an agonised growl. 'Where's *Emmy*?'

CHAPTER FIVE

IT WAS hard to run in oversized rubber boots.

Andrew passed her easily but he didn't see the rabbit hole in the dim evening light and he went sprawling, the heartfelt curse following Alice as she kept running towards the sound of her dog raising the alarm. She knew what lay in that direction.

The river.

She could hear it as she got rapidly closer. There was a shallow stretch where it tumbled swiftly over boulders before it hit the curve shaded by willow trees. There was a deep pool in that curve—a swimming hole that Alice had enjoyed using many times over the recent long, hot summer.

Jake appeared to be standing in the choppy swirl of the shallow water. He had stopped barking now and, as Alice got even closer, she could see why. He had his jaws clamped onto a piece of clothing as he held onto a small body that was no longer upright.

Oh, *God*! Alice charged full tilt into the river and promptly slipped on one of the smooth, wet boulders. Heedless of the painful bump to her knee and the icy water now drenching her clothes, she wrenched herself upright and staggered on.

Too late!

The current had been too much for Jake to fight and now he was bounding down river, following the shape that was Emmy, being swept towards the deep pool. Alice went after them, so fast she was already losing her balance as the water got deeper. Deep enough to swim as she fell headlong into it.

Jake was swimming too. If he hadn't been circling at that particular point beneath the willows, Alice would have had no clue where to dive when Emmy's head suddenly vanished.

The water was pitch-black. There were branches of willow, long enough to trail well below the surface and create both an obstacle to finding the child quickly and a dangerous trap that could entangle and drown Emmy in a very short space of time.

Somehow, Alice's hand found something far more solid than leafy twigs. She gripped and pulled and filled her arms with the child before kicking desperately towards the surface of the pool and then downstream to when the water got shallow again. She staggered upright as soon as her feet touched the bottom.

Strong arms came around them both then, guiding them to the side and onto dry ground. For a split second they stopped moving and Alice could feel more than strength in those arms. They created a circle of protection. A place that felt so safe it took her breath away.

Or was she still holding it from that dive into the deep pool? It had all happened so fast. That moment of stillness vanished with the same speed as Andrew pulled Emmy from her arms.

Oh, dear Lord, was the little girl still breathing?

Yes. Not only breathing, Emmy was sobbing now, her arms wrapped around her father's neck so tightly it was a wonder he could still breathe himself.

'It's okay, honey. Shh…you're all right. You're safe.'

The words were a little broken, the overload of relief so obvious it brought tears to Alice's eyes. How many parents would have spoken in anger in the emotional backwash of something being done that shouldn't have been done? Especially when it had led to a life-threatening situation. But these words held no hint of anger. They were pure reassurance. They were a thick cloak of comfort and a promise of protection.

This child meant everything to Andrew, didn't she? He would have risked his own life in a heartbeat to save her. But, if it hadn't been for Jake, this scene could well have been very, very different. Alice began to shake. She was frozen, of course, soaked with icy water, but part of her reaction was knowing how close they had come to tragedy. Jake was a hero! She turned to see her big dog vigorously shaking the water from his shaggy coat and then he looked up at his mistress, his tail waving slowly.

The tears on Alice's face were invisible, thanks to the water still streaming from her hair. She crouched and hugged Jake. Andrew was using one hand to pull open the jacket he was wearing so he could cover Emmy but he was looking down.

'Jake …' His voice cracked and he stopped speaking.

Alice saw the way his eyes squeezed shut and the muscles in his face fought for control. She tried to smile, to tell him that he didn't need to say anything. She understood.

More, she had to take part of the blame for leaving Emmy unsupervised for long enough to get into trouble. She was the one who'd pulled out the verbal trick that had been nasty enough to distract Andrew.

She couldn't smile. Her teeth were chattering so hard she could barely speak.

'Y-you'd…b-be-better g-get Em-my home. D-dry…'

'Come with us,' Andrew said. 'I'll have a fire going in no time. Hot soup.'

'N-no.' Alice shook her head, the movement jerky. She wrapped her arms around herself tightly because she was shivering so violently it felt as if she might actually fall over. 'W-we're g-good.'

And they were. Her pot belly stove had been alight since before she'd begun hanging the washing out and the cottage would be as warm as toast. She had a pile of old towels in the wash house and she could dry Jake off while her bathtub was filling with lovely hot water. They all needed to move now, however, before the chill of a frosty night really set in.

By tacit consent they all started walking. Emmy had stopped crying but her head was buried against Andrew's shoulder and the rest of her was covered by the padded anorak. Her father was talking to her. Reassuring her as his long legs covered the ground at a speed that left Alice and Jake lagging behind.

He didn't seem to notice when she turned towards the cottage. He kept going towards the big house, striding away with his precious burden, totally focused on getting his daughter home and safe.

And that was fine. Perfectly understandable. No doubt he would thank Alice when she saw him at work tomorrow. He might even feel grateful enough to give her a little more time to find a new place to live.

Or not. It was blatantly obvious he needed assistance in caring for his child until she learned the boundaries of what was acceptable behaviour in her new and exciting environment.

Alice was so cold by the time her bath was ready it was hard enough to turn the taps off, let alone peel still-soaked clothes from her body. A curious exhaustion had also set in and the physical effort of tugging free the skin-tight jodhpurs was almost too much. They rolled themselves into a noose around her ankles so she was forced to sit on the bathroom floor. Every time she tried to force the roll of fabric over her heels, either her stiff fingers refused to cooperate or her arms began to ache with the effort.

Jake was lying on the rug in front of the pot belly stove, happily soaking in its warmth as he finished drying. Alice was alone in her tiny bathroom. Isolated in this small cottage. What if she couldn't get the damn jodhpurs off and she was left getting more and more exhausted and hypothermic? If she tried to get up she might fall and hit her head on the side of the old claw foot bath and then she'd have a head injury as well as hypothermia and she might die!

Alone.

How long would it take Andrew to bother coming to the cottage to find out why she'd disappeared? Three weeks, maybe? Until the date she was supposed to have left the premises?

Stupid tears prickled and Alice was so close to simply giving in to them. It took enormous strength to give herself a decent mental shake.

'Don't be so *ridiculous*,' she said aloud.

She put the ball of one foot against the stubborn roll of fabric on the other ankle, braced herself against the wall and pushed. Hard. It worked, on both sides. It was much easier to peel off the soggy woollen socks and the rest of her clothing, apart from an extended struggle with the catch on her bra, but finally she could climb into the deep bath of gently steaming water.

At first, the heat stung her overly cold skin but after a few minutes it began to seep in to warm her flesh. Some time later, after a top-up from the hot tap, it felt as if her bones were thawing at last and her fingers recovered enough to cope with getting the lid open on her shampoo bottle. Alice soaped her hair and then held her breath and submerged herself to rinse the soap clear.

The horror of what had almost happened in the river was receding and she could finally relax and soak in the warm water now scented with the almond essence from her shampoo. She was safe. Emmy was safe, thank God.

More than safe. As the tension was washed away, Alice was taken back to that tiny moment of time when she'd been held, along with the child, in Andrew's fierce embrace. It had given her just a glimpse of what it would be like to be that...*loved*.

And it made her want to cry. Yet again. What on earth was happening to her? Alice Palmer didn't faint in the face of shocking events. She didn't cry, either. She dealt with things. Made the best of whatever life threw at her and moved on. The way she'd learned to from such an early age when her parents had died and she had been sent to live with first her gran and then boarding schools. She'd moved on from relationships and jobs and places to live that hadn't worked out so why was she feeling so unsettled now?

Where had this new poignant ache in her heart sprung from?

Because she'd never been loved the way Andrew loved Emmy?

Yet, she amended firmly. Okay, it hadn't happened so far but surely there was someone out there who could love her like that? One day. Someone who would trust her and care about her and want to protect her and...

...and be there if she got her trousers stuck around her ankles and hit her head on the side of the bath!

Dismayed at the way she seemed intent on pulling herself down, Alice tugged the plug from the bath and climbed out. She dried herself, wrapped her hair in a towel and then put on the warmest pair of pyjamas she could find. The dark blue ones with yellow stars and moons all over them. Ancient flannelette things her gran had given her years ago. A dressing gown was not something Alice had ever bothered acquiring, but Gran's shawl decorated the back of the small couch in her sitting room so she wrapped that around her shoulders to sit in front of the stove and comb conditioner through her hair.

A long and boring chore, given its length, but it was essential if she wanted to keep any kind of control over her curls. And it was relaxing once the worst of the tangles were gone. Alice kept combing, hoping the heat would dry it quickly. Again and again she pulled the wide-toothed comb from her crown to the ends of her hair that reached almost to her waist. The action, combined with the warmth of the stove, was hypnotic. She had no idea how long she sat there. Or when she dropped the comb into her lap. Or how her arms had gone around herself again in an unconscious, tactile reminder of what was filling her mind.

That moment.

The desire to not only be loved by someone that much but to be loved by someone like Andrew.

No. *By* Andrew himself.

Fantasy was another drug. Powerful and compelling. So consuming that when Jake's head rose sharply and he emitted a low warning growl Alice leapt to her feet, allowing no time to remind herself how safe she knew this haven to be. The comb clattered to the wooden floorboards and the shawl slipped from her shoulders as her heart started to pound. The knock on the door a second or two later echoed the thumping behind her ribs.

'It's okay, Jake,' she said reassuringly. 'I know who it is.'

There was only one person it could be at this time of night, on a property that was so far away from any main roads. But why had he come? Was something wrong with Emmy? Was she showing some nasty after-effect from her near drowning? Aspiration pneumonia, perhaps?

Alice pulled open the door, letting in a blast of frosty air and revealing a slightly out-of-breath man.

'What is it?' she questioned. 'What's wrong?'

'Nothing.' Andrew's breath was coming out in white puffs.

'But you've been running!'

'I don't want to leave Em for too long.'

'Is she all right?'

'She's fine. Fast asleep.' Andrew held up what looked like a walkie-talkie radio. 'I'm well within range if she wakes up and calls and it only took me ninety seconds to run here.'

'But...*why*?'

'I had to come.' Andrew was wearing his jacket but his hands were bare. He rubbed them together, obviously cold. The night air was still rushing into the cottage and Alice was suddenly aware of the nip on her bare toes.

She shivered. 'You'd better come in, then.'

Andrew hesitated for a moment. He was staring at her loose, still damp hair. His gaze travelled to her bare feet and must have taken in the pyjamas on the way.

'I'm sorry. It didn't occur to me that you might be getting ready for bed.'

'I'm not.' Alice tried to ignore the heat her cheeks were generating. 'I haven't even had dinner yet. Look, come in. I need to shut this door before we turn my house into a fridge.'

Alice stepped back and Andrew followed. She shut the door. Jake eyed their visitor with deep suspicion.

'I had to come and thank you,' Andrew said solemnly. 'And Jake.'

He looked down at the dog glued to Alice's leg and then, to her astonishment, he crouched so that his face was level with Jake's.

'You saved Emmy,' he told the dog. 'You are the best dog in the entire world.'

Jake looked up, caught the approving curl of Alice's lips and then he eyed Andrew again. His tail waved in a single wag. Andrew held out his hand and Jake stretched his neck to sniff his fingers. The tail moved again and Alice felt the chill as her dog deserted her leg to step closer to Andrew and accept a scratch behind his ears.

Alice stepped closer to the stove. She eyed the shawl puddle on the floor but it was embarrassing enough to be caught wearing old night-sky pyjamas. To don a homemade, multi-coloured creation would be even more bizarre.

'And you.' Andrew straightened with an easy, smooth motion. He walked towards Alice and held out his hand again. '*You* saved my daughter.'

How weird, to be offered a handshake. Except, when Alice accepted, her hand wasn't shaken. Andrew took it in both of his and clasped it firmly.

'There are no words,' he said softly, 'that could tell you how grateful I am.'

He didn't need words. Alice could feel it. Like a miniature version of the circle his arms had created earlier. And she could feel her eyes widening with the wonder of it. The *power*.

She couldn't hold his gaze because it was too much. The longing that stirred deep within her was so sharp it was unbearable. She had to break the contact. To look away and pull her hand free.

'There's no need to say anything,' she managed. 'I…understand.' She dragged in a new breath. 'And I need to apologise. It would never have happened if I hadn't said what I did and—'

'No,' Andrew interrupted. 'I—'

Alice shook her head, overriding the interruption. She had to finish what she was saying.

'And I wouldn't have done it. I was upset but I hate gossip even if it's true. There's no way I would spread rumours that I know have no basis in truth.'

She risked another glance at Andrew to find him looking startled. As though what she'd just said was hard to take in. His steady gaze was penetrating.

'Thank you,' he said slowly. After a long pause, he spoke again. 'And I need to tell you that I never believed you took those drugs. But—'

He seemed to be struggling to find an explanation. Or possibly an apology, but it wasn't necessary. Alice could see how sincere he was and she could feel the weight of mistrust already starting to slide from her shoulders.

'You did what you had to do at the time,' she offered. 'I understand.'

Her acceptance didn't seem to be enough, however. Andrew was frowning now. He opened his mouth but, instead of him making a sound, the radio transmitter in his hand crackled into life. They both heard a tiny muffled cry and then some words, too mumbled to be comprehensible.

'She's just talking in her sleep,' Andrew said.

But that intent look had gone from his face. His attention was diverted.

'Maybe you should go back,' Alice suggested. 'In case she's waking up.'

The single nod confirmed that she had read Andrew's thoughts, but he hesitated as Alice opened her door, in the same way he had before coming in. She thought he was about to say something else, but then he simply gave her another nod and disappeared into the night.

The braid was back again this morning, of course, but Andrew couldn't look at that rope of hair without thinking of how it had looked last night, cascading over Alice's shoulders in a ripple of deep chestnut with copper sparkles from the light. Hopefully, the awareness was mainly due to having to think about hair on his patient.

Seven-year-old Sean had ridden his bike under a low-hanging tree branch and given himself a decent scalp laceration. Andrew was using hair ties rather than sutures to close it. He selected just a few hairs on each side of the cut and tied the first half of the knot to draw the skin together.

'Bit of glue, thanks, Alice.'

She leaned closer to dab a spot of tissue adhesive to the top of the knot. 'You're being very good, keeping still like this, Sean.' Then she caught her bottom lip between her teeth as she glanced up. 'You didn't want gloves?'

Andrew shook his head as he completed the knot. 'There's no bleeding now.' He started the procedure again at the centre of the laceration. 'And it's too hard to pick up tiny bunches of hair with gloves on. I can't feel it properly.'

Explaining his lack of basic personal protection equipment was enough to make him more aware of the feel of the child's hair between his fingers.

Enough to make him wonder whether Alice's hair would feel this silky. Not that he'd want to be holding a piece the size of fishing line, mind you. No. He'd want to bury his fingers in it and crumple it against her head while he positioned it perfectly in order to meet his kiss.

'Will it hurt?'

'Sorry?' What Andrew had flitting through the back of his mind wasn't likely to hurt at all. Quite the opposite!

'When he combs his hair?' Sean's mother was looking anxious.

Andrew finished the last knot. 'He'll need to be careful not to catch the knots with the comb. Don't wash his hair for five days and, when you do, just rub gently over the knots. If they're still there in ten days, you can cut them out.'

'Can I have a bandage?' Sean asked.

'You don't need one,' Alice told him. 'We put special glue on that's going to keep it nice and clean. Like superglue.'

'You superglued my head back together? Cool!'

'You can tell them all about it at school.' Andrew smiled. 'No headache?'

'Nah, I'm good. Can I ride my bike again later?'

'Only if you're wearing your helmet,' his mother said with a sigh. 'Like you're *supposed* to do.'

Sean was still looking up at his doctor. 'What she said.' Andrew nodded. 'You be careful out there, young man. Stop giving your mum frights like that.'

Alice was nodding her agreement. She'd seen how pale Sean's mother had been on arrival, still pressing a blood-stained towel to her son's head. She turned to

Andrew as Sean left the cubicle and the message in her eyes was as clear as if she'd spoken aloud.

Emmy's safe now, it said. Try not to dwell on it.

The message stayed with him as he moved onto his next patient. Yes, Emmy was safe, but he couldn't remember that without remembering what Alice had done without a moment's hesitation—hurling herself into that river to rescue his daughter. She'd read his mind back there in Sean's cubicle, too. His blood still ran cold, imagining what could have happened.

The horrific thoughts had kept him awake for much of last night. Along with the way Alice's apology had made him feel.

Humble.

No. Make that ashamed.

It was a minute or two's walk to get to the woman with abdominal pain who was now in the observation area but needed reassessment, and it gave Andrew a small window of time to think about it yet again. To try and justify his actions.

Okay, he'd told her he'd never believed she'd taken those drugs and that was good but he'd stopped short of telling her he *knew* she hadn't.

He wanted to, but he couldn't.

If there was any way he could prevent it, Andrew was never going to have anyone look at Emmy differently because her mother had been a drug addict. No one. Instinct told him that it would make no difference to Alice but he couldn't guarantee that, could he? He couldn't guarantee that she would never mention it to anyone else and, however small that risk was, it was one he really wasn't prepared to take.

History seemed to be repeating itself in so many ways. Inadequate care for Emmy. A blackmail attempt by a woman. Doing what he had to do at the time. It had been the potential risk to others of being wrong that had made him unable to support Alice's innocence regarding those missing drugs. It was exactly the same as not telling her the entire story now. He was protecting Emmy.

Alice would understand that last one if she ever found out, but why would she? He'd insisted on complete confidentiality from all medical personnel involved with Melissa's treatment and the files were now out of circulation for ever.

The subject need never come up because he was just as prepared as Alice seemed to be to put the past and all its rumours behind them. They had a new bond now, through Emmy.

A bond that seemed destined to become stronger. Mid-afternoon, a trauma case came in that needed full-on attention. Andrew couldn't leave the bedside of the man with a head injury from being knocked off his motorbike. He had to ask Alice to go and get whatever urgent message someone was trying to leave him by phone.

She came back as the staff had stepped away from the centre of the resuscitation area to allow X-rays to be taken of the patient's neck, chest and pelvis.

'It's the after-school care facility,' she informed Andrew. 'Emmy's running a bit of a temperature and has a runny nose. They think she should be taken home.'

Andrew stared through the heavy glass protecting them from an unwanted dose of radioactivity. 'I can't leave right now.' He rubbed the back of his neck. 'It's probably just a cold.'

Alice was nodding but he could see the concern in her face.

'I'll get away as soon as I can but my shift doesn't end till six.' And he was needed again now. The X-ray technicians had finished. His patient needed treatment.

'I'm finished now,' Alice said. 'I could pick Emmy up and take her home if you like.'

The offer was too good to pass up. 'Are you sure?'

'Yes. I'd like to make sure she's all right. After yesterday.'

'Bring her in here if you're at all worried.'

'I will. Otherwise, I'll take her home.'

'Grab my key. They're on the desk in my office. The house key is the big, old one. I'll see you as soon as I can.'

'Don't rush. We'll be fine.' Alice was on her way out of the room.

'Alice?'

She turned back.

'Thank you.'

The fact that Andrew had accepted her offer of help with childcare had been unexpected.

He might not be able to tell her she was worthy of his trust, but actions spoke louder than words and this was a loud shout.

It hadn't been a grudging acceptance because he had no choice, either. He'd thanked her, when it would have been perfectly acceptable to have turned his attention immediately back to his patient. And not only had he thanked her; Alice had been treated to a glimmer of one of *those* smiles.

Directed at herself!

It gave her a warm glow that might have negated the need to build a fire if it hadn't been for poor little Emmy. The girl had red cheeks and overbright eyes and her nose was dripping like a tap. Her chest was clear, however, and her temperature only slightly raised. She wasn't sick enough for it to be any more than a mild viral infection.

'We're going to give you some paracetamol and then a lovely warm bath,' Alice told her charge. 'Have you got pyjamas and slippers and a dressing gown?'

Emmy nodded. 'Are you going to be my nanny now?'

'Just for today, hon. Till Daddy gets home.'

'Coz I'm sick?'

'That's right.' Alice led the way into the kitchen to measure out the liquid paracetamol she'd brought from work. She lifted Emmy to sit on the old scrubbed pine table while she opened drawers to find a spoon.

'I like being sick,' Emmy announced.

'*Do* you?'

'Yes.' Her small face was screwed up in distaste while the anti-inflammatory medicine was swallowed but then Emmy smiled at Alice. 'I think I'm going to be sick for a long time.'

'No, it's just a cold, hon. You'll be as right as rain in a day or two.' Emmy's scowl made her raise her eyebrows. 'You don't *want* to be sick for a long time, do you?'

'Yes, I do.'

'Why?'

'Coz you'll look after me.'

'Ohh.' Alice lifted the child down and then took her hand as they left the kitchen.

Oh, help. Emmy sure knew how to climb right into someone's heart, didn't she? Andrew had made a valid point the other day. Getting attached would make it much harder when she had to leave. For both Emmy and herself.

Maybe this hadn't been such a brilliant idea. Except this was the first time she'd stepped inside this wonderful old house and Alice had to admit she was fascinated.

'Where's the bathroom, hon?'

'Up the stairs. C'mon, I'll show you.'

Alice was being tugged along by one hand. She ran the other up the smooth banister of golden wood, where each rail beneath was intricately carved with vines and flowers. Brass rods held a faded oriental-style carpet in place, which seamlessly extended to run the length of the gallery at the top.

'This is my room.'

There were shelves full of books and toys scattered on the floor. A doll's house in one corner and a blackboard easel where Emmy's name had been beautifully written in different coloured chalks, presumably by her father. Alice turned her head and had to catch her breath.

'You've got a four-poster bed!'

'Daddy told them to leave it in the house. He said it was for me coz I'm his princess.'

Alice touched the drapes of white muslin. 'It's beautiful.'

'I like it...' Emmy nodded '...but I like Daddy's better.'

'Oh?' Alice moved again in response to new tugging. She knew where Emmy was leading her now and had to squash the frisson of guilt that the thought of seeing Andrew's bedroom gave her. She shouldn't be doing this.

Emmy trotted ahead, looking less unwell by the moment, but wiping her nose on her other sleeve. She let go of Alice's hand and climbed onto a much more ordinary-looking bed that had plain, dark wooden ends.

'Why do you like it more than yours?' Alice tried not to look around, but she couldn't help seeing the crumpled shirt in the corner and the handful of coins carelessly dumped on the chest of drawers.

'Coz Daddy's in here.' Emmy sounded as though Alice should have already known that, but she'd been more successful in trying not to think about it than looking around the room, hadn't she?

Trying not to imagine him with his head on those pillows, sprawled across what was a very large space for one person to sleep in. Wearing...what, just pyjama pants and nothing else? She turned away quickly. What if Emmy later told her father how red Alice's face had gone when she'd been in his room?

'Bath time,' she said firmly. 'And then we're going to make a fire and some dinner and you can find all your favourite stories for me to read to you.'

'When's Daddy coming home?'

'When he's finished at work.'

'Before bedtime?'

'I should think so. What time do you have to go to bed?'

Emmy's eyes might be too bright to be healthy but they hadn't lost their determined glint. 'When Daddy tells me to.'

He was a lot later than he'd wanted to be. It had taken time to sort all his patients enough to be happy to transfer their care, and it was after 7:00 p.m. by the time Andrew made it home. He was tired enough to be thinking it was crazy to be living this far from town.

Yesterday's scare with Emmy, a virtually sleepless night and a full-on day with the extra worry of how unwell Emmy might be adding more tension to the last few hours had drained him utterly. His briefcase felt like a lead weight as he dropped it by the hall stand. He pulled off his jacket and snagged it onto a hook and then turned to move towards the kitchen end of the vast hallway.

Something felt very different from the previous times he'd arrived home here. Was it the delicious aroma coming from the kitchen? The warmth he could feel from the slightly ajar doorway that led to the old library? Or was it what he could see in the soft glow of lamplight when he pushed that door open?

Alice sat on one end of a couch, holding a book she was reading from, with her other arm around the lumpy shape that was Emmy all bundled up in a duvet.

Maybe it was because he was exhausted and hungry and worried about his daughter that made this scene seem poignant enough to make his throat constrict painfully. Or maybe it was a combination of this and the warmth and the smell of food. It made him feel as if he'd actually come *home* for the first time he could remember since being a child himself.

Alice stopped reading as he moved further into the room. She smiled but said nothing.

Andrew looked at the still shape beside her. 'Is she okay?'

'Sound asleep,' Alice said softly. 'She had her dinner an hour ago and another dose of paracetamol about thirty minutes ago. I put a hot-water bottle in her bed.'

'I'll take her up.'

He had to bend down to gather Emmy and the duvet into his arms, which put him close enough to feel the warmth of Alice and to imagine what it had been like for Emmy, cuddled against her and listening to her voice reading a story as she drifted to sleep.

It would have felt like home. Like having a real mother for the first time in her short life.

Just as well he had to leave the room and attend to his daughter. Andrew needed time to shake off this odd sensation that he suddenly had regarding Alice Palmer—that he no longer wanted to evict her.

That he wanted… needed to keep her in his life somehow.

He came back downstairs to find her taking a hot meal from the oven for him. A rich-smelling beef casserole and baked potatoes. Homely comfort food.

'Have *you* eaten?'

She nodded. 'I had some with Emmy.'

'Would you like a glass of wine? I think this—' he looked down at the plate of food on the table '—deserves the best red I can find.' He reached into the wine rack beside the old Aga stove and then turned to search a drawer for a corkscrew.

'I...shouldn't. Jake will be wondering where *his* dinner is.'

'Please...stay for a few minutes.' Andrew pulled out a chair. 'I need to thank you properly and I want to ask about how Emmy's been, but if I don't eat I might fall over in a huge heap. Lunch was so long ago I can't even remember whether I ate it.'

Alice sat but it was on the edge of her chair. Andrew put two glasses and the open wine bottle in front of her. 'Could you carry these, please?'

Now she looked really nervous. 'Where to?'

'To enjoy that lovely fire you made.' He picked up his plate. 'Coming?'

'Just for a minute or two.' The agreement sounded deliberate. 'There is something I'd like to talk to you about.'

He didn't find out what that something was until he'd eaten his whole plateful of that delicious food. Until he was warm and full and quite happy with what Alice had been telling him about Emmy's condition. The wine was also contributing to making him feel extraordinarily good.

'What was it,' he enquired, 'that you wanted to talk to me about?'

'Childcare.' Alice got up from the other couch to put another log on the fire.

'Ohh.' The sound was a groan. 'Ringing the agency was on my list for today but I didn't get a spare minute. Thank you again for your help. I don't know how I'd have managed without it.'

'It was no trouble,' Alice said quietly. 'I...enjoyed it. Emmy's a delight.'

'You didn't have to go the extra mile like this.' Andrew set his empty plate on the floor by his feet.

'It was an idea I had,' Alice said slowly. She was still kneeling beside the fireplace. 'I wanted to show you rather than just talk about it.'

Show him? Andrew's head felt a little fuzzy. Had to be the wine because he was looking at her kneeling there with the firelight playing on her hair and face and he thought she was talking about making the fire and dinner and caring for his child. Being a homemaker. A mother to Emmy. A...a *wife*?

And, God help him, but the idea was very, very appealing.

'I could be a nanny,' he heard Alice saying. 'And...a kind of housekeeper. It could work, if I juggled my shifts a bit so I did nights or weekends when you weren't on call.'

'Why would you want to do that? What's in it for you?'

'My home,' Alice said simply. 'I wouldn't want to be paid or anything. I'd just like to keep living in the cottage and you said you needed it for someone who would help with Emmy and things. I can do that. I'd *like* to do it. What...what do you think?'

What did he think? Andrew was aware of a ridiculous wash of disappointment that his tired brain had come up with entirely the wrong scenario. This was a business deal, nothing more.

Except...it could be more. They already had a bond of a past they didn't want to share with others. And a new bond through Emmy. This arrangement could give them a new base. An opportunity for each of them to provide something the other wanted instead of a threat of removing something. A positive spin on a situation they both needed to deal with.

A fresh start, even.

'It might work,' he said slowly. 'But…'

'…But?' Alice's eyes were huge. Fixed on him.

Andrew found himself leaning closer. 'But we'd have to trust each other.' And that was a problem, wasn't it? Hadn't he sworn never to trust another woman after what Melissa had put him through?

'I trust *you*,' Alice said softly. 'Do you think you can trust me?'

She didn't break the eye contact and Andrew was close enough now to see the flecks of gold in her eyes as the flames beside her flickered. He could see the tangle of dark lashes around them and the pale, smooth skin of her face. He could hear the hitch of her breath. Or was that his own?

How come he'd never noticed before that she was such an extraordinarily beautiful woman? A man could fall into eyes like those and not even want to save himself from drowning. It was all he could do not to lean further forward and touch her lips with his own.

'Yes,' he heard himself saying a little raggedly. 'I know I can.'

CHAPTER SIX

IT WAS enough.

That he trusted her and that she could keep the home she loved.

That she didn't have to try and achieve the impossible and make herself hate him.

This was a trial period but, even if Alice hadn't been so determined to make it work, it became rapidly clear that her idea had been brilliant. A bit of juggling was needed in the early days, but their colleagues were willing to help ensure that their shifts didn't clash and that one of them always had their days off on weekends. A routine was established with such astonishing ease it was hard for Alice not to think that this was meant to be happening.

That finally, for the first time in her life, the planets were aligning themselves exactly the way she would have dreamed.

On a day shift, Alice headed to work early and Andrew got Emmy ready for school and dropped her into the care centre on his way to work. Alice would finish at 3:00 p.m. and could get to school to collect

Emmy without her needing after school care. They would shop for groceries if needed on the way home and Alice would help Emmy with her homework, do housework like washing or ironing and then prepare dinner.

Caring for her pets was not an issue. Emmy was only too keen to visit Ben and help groom and feed him and Jake was more than welcome in the house where he would always have hero status.

If Alice had an afternoon shift, she took Emmy to school in the morning and Andrew collected her on his way home. She was more than prepared to put the extra effort into her side of this bargain. Especially when Andrew refused to take any further rent for her cottage or grazing land.

'You have no idea, do you,' he said to silence her protests, 'how much this will be worth to me if it works?'

And it *was* working, even with nights shifts factored in. When Alice had a night shift, she looked after Emmy in the morning and slept while the little girl was at school and when Andrew had to be at the hospital over-night she slept in the big house.

That first morning was a little awkward, certainly, when Andrew arrived home to find her making an early morning cup of tea in the kitchen, still in her pyjamas, but moments of discomfort like that wore off re-markably quickly. Or got dispensed with. Like Alice leaving to go back to the cottage when Andrew arrived home in the evenings to the meal she had prepared.

'Don't be daft,' he told her during the second week. 'You don't need to cook twice. Three times if you count feeding Emmy early. Stay and eat with me.'

If Emmy was still up, they would take their plates of food and eat in front of the fire and sometimes Emmy was allowed to toast marshmallows. If she was asleep, they would eat at the kitchen table. Being alone with each other in front of a fire would have been stepping over an unspoken boundary. This was, after all, an arrangement that happened to suit them both. No more than a second job for Alice. It had nothing to do with a more personal relationship.

Conversation was limited to either Emmy or work. By another tacit agreement, there was a boundary on a timeline. They didn't talk about the time they had worked together previously and they never stepped further back than that to learn anything about families or growing up. It was as if a completely new start was being made and it was either too early or inappropriate to venture into personal space.

And it was enough.

Too much, perhaps.

Given how well things were working, it was inevitable that somewhere along the way in those first weeks hope was born again.

And it blossomed.

Maybe it was the softening Alice saw in Andrew's face as the tension of making this new life work lessened. The smile that accompanied the appreciation he never failed to communicate. Or perhaps it was the day when they both happened to have a Saturday off work and Andrew had knocked at the door of the cottage mid-morning, with Emmy clinging to his hand and beaming triumphantly.

'We were wondering,' Andrew said, 'whether you might be available for a trip into town.'

He was wearing his faded jeans and a warm jersey, his dark blond hair a little more tousled than it ever looked at work, and Alice realised that any downside of this arrangement and the subsequent shift juggling that meant seeing less of him in the emergency department was more than made up for by seeing him like this in his role as a father and on his home ground. Being privileged enough to share a part of his private life.

Quite apart from the smile currently deepening the grooves on his cheeks and making the corners of his eyes crinkle. A smile that could easily persuade Alice she would be available for a trip to the moon if he happened to be asking.

Emmy was bouncing with excitement. 'For shopping,' she informed Alice. 'For *me*.'

'Em's a bit short on clothes and shoes and things,' Andrew added. 'And…um…you're a girl.'

'Like *me*!' Emmy crowed.

'And…as it's been pointed out to me more than once this morning, I'm not.'

'No…you're not…' Alice was caught. Falling into the blue eyes of the man on her doorstep. Eyes that told her she wasn't a girl at all. That she was a woman and that Andrew was a mere male. And that he was as aware of the implications of that as she was.

And Alice knew she was lost. That she would always *be* lost unless—until—Andrew found her.

She was here. She would always be here. When he was ready and if he chose to find her, it would be so easy.

'I'd love to come shopping,' was all she could say.

* * *

It was at moments like this that Andrew had to remind himself very firmly that this was merely a business arrangement. That Alice was doing this because she needed accommodation for herself and her pets.

The problem was, it was working so well that at odd moments, Andrew was inclined to forget. Like now, with Emmy on her booster seat in the back and Alice in the front passenger seat of his car as they made their way into the city for the shopping expedition.

Somehow, over the period of about a month, Alice had become such an integral part of their lives that he couldn't imagine her not being here.

He'd been singing along with both of them to some silly song about caterpillars that was on Emmy's favourite CD but he trailed into silence that nobody seemed to notice. It was a sparkling winter's day with the clearest blue sky he'd ever seen and a breathtaking view of the Southern Alps with a good coating of snow. And his daughter sounded so happy Andrew found himself smiling.

Then he glanced to his left, to where Alice was sitting there in her jeans and a soft-looking jumper in a shade of deep russet…just like the loose braid of hair that fell over her shoulder. She was gamely trying to keep up with a chorus that involved a lot of numbers to do with caterpillar legs and she was using her fingers to try and keep track. Slim, capable, elegant fingers and hands that were a perfect match for the rest of her body.

A body that Andrew was finding increasingly attractive. An attraction Andrew couldn't give in to because he would be risking a status quo that was—almost—perfect.

His smile faded as he found himself wishing away

the past. Wishing that he could be the man he used to be—untainted by a past that had destroyed such a big part of his heart.

Wishing that he'd noticed her properly all those years ago instead of being blinded by Melissa's charms and the flattery of being apparently adored. Before his ability to trust at that level had been damaged beyond repair.

But if he wished all that away, it would mean Emmy wouldn't exist and she was the sun in his universe. His first adult experience of unconditional, reciprocated love. The need to cherish and protect his daughter had flickered into life the moment he'd held his newborn in his arms and the flame only burned more brightly as the years had gone by.

No. He couldn't do anything that would pose a threat to this arrangement that was ensuring Emmy's well-being and happiness. Alice might run a mile if she knew how he was feeling and how hard it was to try and keep his hands off her. He would be abusing a position of power over her as her landlord. Or employer or what-ever role she now saw him as having.

Except... Having to concentrate on the traffic as they made their way into the central city gave Andrew an excuse to let his thoughts wander a little further down that track. Sometimes, he had the impression that Alice might feel the same way. The way she smiled, for example, when he came home from work to a house that was feeling more and more like the home he'd always dreamed of. Or when she seemed to be reluctant to head back to the cottage and leave him to tackle the dishes when he insisted on contributing to the housework. Or like that moment outside her cottage today when he'd told her that Emmy wanted female companionship for the shopping trip.

Was it just wishful thinking that made him imagine a crackle of sexual tension?

If so, he was being an idiot. There was no guarantee that any relationship would work, no matter how eager the participants were. He'd learned that painful lesson very thoroughly. And if he started something that turned to custard it would be far worse for both himself and Emmy when Alice made an exit from their lives. The routine they had going now was making it possible for him to settle into his new job and for Emmy to settle into the huge change of starting school.

She'd grown up so much in the last few weeks. His little girl had left babyhood well behind. Her confidence and determination seemed to grow stronger every day. She certainly knew what she wanted when it came to choosing clothes.

'I want jeans,' she announced. 'Like Alice's. And boots.'

'Boots?'

'You know—the ones with the stretchy bits on the sides.'

'Jodhpur boots,' Alice supplied. 'They are quite practical for being outside on a farm.'

'We won't find them in a shoe shop. Maybe another time, Em. We need to get stuff that's useful for school.'

'I want to wear boots to school.'

'No,' Andrew said firmly. 'Shoes for school. Boots for home.'

'So I can get some boots, then?'

Andrew looked helplessly at Alice but she just grinned. 'There's a saddlery shop not that far away. They do boots.'

They did more than boots. Emmy found a rack of child-sized jodhpurs and she turned a look of such pleading towards her father that he shook his head in defeat.

'Why not? You do sit on Ben quite a lot these days.'

The salesgirl was happy to help find sizes to fit. She found a pair of jodhpurs with suede inserts on the back and insides of the legs.

'Sticky bums,' she told Emmy. 'They help you stay in the saddle.'

She held the toggle on the back of the boots as Emmy excitedly stuffed her feet into a shiny brown pair.

'What's your pony's name?' she asked.

'I haven't got a pony,' Emmy said sadly. 'I sit on Ben but he's too big for me to ride.'

The girl looked up at Andrew. 'If you're interested,' she said, 'I happen to know a small pony that would be perfect for a beginner that's looking for a new home.'

'No, thank you,' Andrew said.

'Oh, yes, *please*!' Emmy said at exactly the same moment.

The salesgirl grinned at Alice. 'The advertisement is on the counter. Maybe Mum gets the casting vote.'

The odd stillness that seemed to freeze time was enough to make the salesgirl blush as she realised she'd said something awkward.

Andrew couldn't say anything. He didn't dare look at Alice. But Emmy, bless her, wasn't in the least perturbed.

'I haven't got a mum,' she said. 'She's dead.'

'Oh...' The salesgirl didn't know where to look. 'I'm so sorry.'

Andrew held his breath. It was the kind of sympathetic response everybody offered and, initially, it had been easy to respond to. He'd been grieving as deeply as any widower. Mourning the fact that any possibility of a meaningful marriage was gone. Sad beyond measure that his daughter would grow up motherless.

But he'd been living with that grief ever since Emmy had been born.

Did Alice think it odd that he never mentioned his wife? Or that there were no photographs on display? Did Emmy ever say anything when he wasn't around? Probably not. She'd been only three years old when Melissa had died and she'd only seen her mother before that during the periods that her mother hadn't been resident in rehab clinics. That her mother was dead was a fact she was happy to relate to anyone, as she had just done to the poor salesgirl.

The bond she should have had with her mother had been Andrew's privilege to receive. Past nannies had been loved but hadn't intruded into that bond.

Until now.

Somehow, Alice had crept in and Andrew had no idea what, if anything, he could or should do about it.

Just like he had no idea how to rescue this salesgirl from her obvious, acute embarrassment.

But Emmy had that in hand as well.

'It's all right,' she told the girl kindly. 'I've got Alice now.'

* * *

The embarrassment over her mistaken identity was still there thirty minutes or more later when Andrew steered them all into a fast food restaurant for lunch.

Had it been an attempt to gloss over the incident that had made him agree to all Emmy's desired purchases in the saddlery? Even to the point of taking a copy of the advertisement for the pony and saying he would think about it?

At least it gave them something to talk about over their hamburgers and fries.

'His name is Paddington Bear,' Alice said in answer to Emmy's query.

'Very English,' Andrew noted. 'In fact, he looks remarkably like a Thelwell pony.'

He did. Paddington was a tiny Shetland with long shaggy hair and a very round belly. According to the information on the advertisement, he also had an unblemished record of being a beloved children's pony for the last eighteen years.

'Isn't that extremely old?' Andrew asked.

'Not really. I've known ponies who are still full of go when they're thirty.' Alice smiled at the photograph. 'He's certainly cute and if he's as quiet as this says, he really could be a perfect first pony.'

Andrew shook his head. 'I don't know anything about keeping ponies.'

'But I do,' Alice said softly.

Emmy was apparently entirely focused on dipping fries into the little sachet of tomato sauce and eating them very, very slowly, like a rabbit nibbling on carrots. Maybe she was hoping that if she kept very quiet and wished very hard the adults involved would make a decision in her favour.

She didn't see the way those adults were looking at each other right now.

'What happens,' Andrew asked slowly, holding Alice's gaze, 'when you go somewhere else?'

Alice had to put down her food. Her appetite vanished as her heart skipped a beat. She couldn't look away from Andrew. What was she seeing in that intense gaze? Some kind of plea? An invitation to reveal what was becoming impossible to hide? She had no control over the silent assurance she knew her gaze was sending.

You can trust me. Always.

'Why would I want to go somewhere else?' was what she tried to say aloud. It came out in little more than a whisper.

Andrew made no audible response to that but something changed.

Something huge.

It felt as though time had frozen again. As though the earth had just tilted on its axis. And then she saw a flicker of warmth in Andrew's eyes that had the effect of generating an astonishing heat. Thank goodness she was sitting down, Alice thought hazily, because she was melting here. She couldn't even feel her legs. Couldn't feel anything below the level of that heat low down in her abdomen.

The silence hung there long enough for Emmy's head to jerk up to reveal a small, anxious face.

Alice could feel the drag as Andrew transferred his gaze to his daughter.

'You had enough to eat, pumpkin? Shall I ring the number on that advertisement and see if Paddington Bear is home for visitors?'

The squeal of excitement from Emmy made heads turn all over the crowded restaurant. This time, Alice and Andrew could exchange a glance and share the embarrassment. Dilute it with understanding and amusement.

The way doting parents could.

And it felt…right.

Alice drew in a very deep breath as she emptied their trays of rubbish into the bin near the door. She let it out in a long, almost relieved sigh.

They'd stepped onto a new road. No. An old road for her. One that she'd been stranded on for a very long time. The difference was that Andrew had joined her. And maybe this time it would lead somewhere. It didn't matter how long it took to take the next steps because stepping onto that road at all was the hardest one to take. You couldn't go backwards and it was only a matter of time before forward movement was inevitable.

And it didn't matter how long that was going to take because Alice had been waiting for years. She was more than happy to keep waiting for as long as it took Andrew to catch up. She fully expected that to takes weeks, if not months.

No way was she prepared for it to take only a matter of hours.

She didn't want to go somewhere else.

She wanted to be here.

With him.

For ever?

Despite every argument his mind wanted to produce for the rest of that amazing day, Andrew couldn't get past the notion that he *could* trust Alice.

He wanted to, dammit! He wanted to trust her, heart and soul. Enough to be able to give and thereby receive the kind of love that could last for ever. He'd given away even the possibility of finding that for himself. Until he'd seen something in Alice's gaze back there in the fast food outlet. Something that had touched him in a place he'd believed didn't exist any more.

He knew, on a rational level, that not all women were like Melissa. Self-centred and deceitful and incapable of taking the feelings of others into consideration. And he knew Alice wasn't anything like that.

But he also knew the agony that believing in someone and being proved wrong time and again could cause. He could deal with it himself if he had to, but he couldn't deal with having to try and explain it to his innocent child. Were they already past the point that she could be protected, though? Emmy trusted Alice completely. Loved her.

Andrew could see it in the way his little girl hung onto Alice's hand and looked to *her* for reassurance when she was sitting on top of one small, fat pony, being led around for a trial ride. He saw the look of pure joy they shared when the trial was deemed complete.

For a moment Andrew felt a pang of...not jealousy exactly. A sadness, almost, in acknowledging that Emmy would find people in this world that could share a bond he couldn't share. Others could give her things she needed that he couldn't provide. Was this a part of parenting? A gradual letting go, a tiny piece at a time? Giving Emmy freedom to explore the world and what others had to offer?

And then Alice bent to whisper something in Emmy's ear and she looked up and smiled as Emmy launched herself to hug her father and suddenly he was included in that joy. A part of a totally new adventure. He hugged Emmy but looked over her shoulder at Alice, aware of something warm and tight in his chest as he tried to thank her with a look.

Something elemental was changing today and it was so much to try and get his head around that Andrew was feeling a little dazed. The easiest course of action was to go with the flow, especially when the current was this strong.

All he had to do was produce his chequebook. Do a lot of driving to go home and collect the horse float and then back to collect the new addition to the family, along with enough accessories to fill the back of Alice's truck. Paddington Bear came with everything he could possibly need. A saddle and bridle and warm coats. Brushes and lead ropes and feed buckets.

Emmy was glowing with excitement.

'Look, Daddy! Ben loves him. They're best friends already.'

It looked ridiculous, the giant black horse and the small hairy pony, but, amazingly, they were grazing nose to nose and looking as though they'd known each other for ever.

Andrew had a mental image of Alice on her horse holding the reins with just one hand. With one of those lead ropes in her other hand attached to a miniature version alongside. His stomach did a slow curl. Could he trust Alice to keep Emmy safe?

He had no choice. He could hardly buy a pony for his daughter and then refuse to allow her to learn to ride.

Could he trust Alice further than that?

The real test came later that evening when Emmy, exhausted by the most exciting day of her life, was soundly asleep.

Alice was insisting on being allowed to help clear up after the dinner they'd shared. She had a tea towel in her hands but Andrew grabbed the other end of the cloth.

'I'll do the dishes,' he said. 'You did most of the cooking.'

'It'll only take a minute.' Alice was smiling as she gave a tug.

Andrew tugged back. Harder. Hard enough to pull Alice closer.

So close, she was right there in front of him, looking up, and suddenly the laughter in her face faded. For a long, long moment they stood in absolute stillness and Andrew found himself sinking. He let his eyes make a slow map of her face. The wispy curls of new hair at her temples. The pale skin and delightful dusting of freckles. Those glorious hazel eyes with their golden flecks. A pretty snub nose that he had an urge to kiss the tip of. And then, at last, her lips. So soft-looking. Parted slightly to look...expectant.

Andrew forgot about kissing the tip of her nose. He bent his head so he could touch her lips with his own.

The softness...the sweetness... The electrifying bolt of desire was startling enough to make Andrew jerk back. He saw the same wonder in Alice's eyes but she didn't move. Didn't try and withdraw from him.

He could feel her breath on his face and see the beat of a rapid pulse in her neck. And then the tip of her tongue appeared to touch her lips where his lips had just been and the magnetic pull back was irresistible.

This time he was ready for that shaft of sensation that went through every cell in his body. He could keep control. To explore every delicious part of Alice's lips and mouth. To experiment with different amounts of pressure and let his tongue dance with hers.

He could slide his fingers into her hair and taste that silky skin on the side of her neck. Let his hands drift lower and discover the curve of her breast. He heard her gasp at the same moment he found the hardness of her nipples beneath the soft wool of her jersey.

And then he had to stop and pull back. While he still had some semblance of control. He was breathing hard and so was Alice. They were back to where they'd started. Standing there, staring at each other. But so much had changed.

'I don't want to stop,' Andrew confessed.

'Neither do I,' Alice whispered.

'I…um…haven't got a condom to my name.'

'Neither do I.' Alice licked her lips again and Andrew stifled a low groan of need. 'I…um…I am on the pill.'

'Oh?' *Why?* Was there—or had there recently been—someone else? Okay, this was jealousy. White-hot.

Alice sensed the unspoken demand and gave her head a tiny shake.

'It's not that…' She caught her breath. 'I haven't been in any kind of relationship for a very long time.'

'Neither have I. More than five years, in fact.' Not since Emmy was conceived, just about. How embarrassing was that? 'Beat that,' he said with a wry smile.

'I just about could.' Alice closed her eyes for a heartbeat. Was she also embarrassed admitting to a lack of any love-life?

Andrew swallowed. 'I've never had an STD.'

'Me neither.' Alice opened her eyes again and he could see that she understood what he was suggesting.

He could also see that she thought he was crazy. He *was* crazy. Except…he'd told her he trusted her but he hadn't when it really mattered, had he? He hadn't stood up for her in the face of those allegations about the drugs and she'd ended up losing everything. Her job. Her home. Probably most of her friends.

Going this far in the trust stakes now was like…an apology. A way of putting things right.

Maybe something of what he was thinking was being communicated to Alice because she blinked slowly and when he could see her eyes again he could see that the shock of suggestion was wearing off.

'We did all have to get tested for HIV after that patient bled everywhere in Emergency.'

'I was clear.'

'Me, too.'

So there it was. A desire that seemed equally intense on both sides. A clean bill of health and protection against pregnancy, if what Alice told him was the truth.

It was a question of trust. A huge amount of trust, but Andrew found he didn't need to even think about it any longer. He had an obligation to carry this through.

'I trust you, Alice,' he said slowly. 'Do you trust me?'

'Yes.'

He touched her face, softly trailing a finger from her brow, around her eye, across her cheekbone and finally to brush it across her lips.

'I want you, Alice Palmer.'

She didn't have to say anything. Her answer was in her eyes. In the way she mirrored his action and reached up to touch *his* face. In the way she released her breath in a sigh that held just the edge of a whimper of desire.

Andrew dropped his hand. He laced his fingers through hers and when he moved, she was right beside him. All the way up the stairs.

Into his bedroom.

CHAPTER SEVEN

'So…YOU and Andy Barrett.'

'Mmm.'

Jo eyed her friend with a mixture of respect and envy. 'Lucky you!'

'Mmm.'

'How long has it been going on for?' Jo was setting out the last plastic tray of the sushi she had brought in to share for lunch.

'Oh…a few weeks.'

'And you never said anything!'

'No.' Alice stirred some wasabi into the little pot of soy sauce and then dribbled it over a roll that had a delicious-looking mixture of chicken and avocado. 'I was…it was…'

Too precious to share. Too unbelievably good to be true. Alice had spent the last weeks expecting to wake up and find she was dreaming it all.

Jo was smiling as if she understood. For a moment, the two women ate in silence in the otherwise deserted staff room and then Jo glanced up.

'He's got a little girl, hasn't he?'

'Yes, Emmy. She's five.'

'And that's okay?'

'Better than okay. She's gorgeous.' Alice reached for another roll. 'These are great.'

'Leftovers from dinner last night. My flatmate was celebrating and went a bit overboard on the ordering.'

Alice swallowed her mouthful. 'Emmy's got a pony now. I'm teaching her to ride. She's such a gutsy little kid, she wants to get rid of the lead rein and be galloping over the hills already.'

'Sounds like a match made in heaven.'

'Mmm.' Alice couldn't help the smile that just kept growing.

It would have been enough that she and Andrew were now lovers and that the private times they had together were far more wonderful than any fantasy she had conjured up in the past. What made it breathtaking and had stolen her heart completely had been the way Andrew had trusted her.

She'd told him she was on the pill and protected from the risk of pregnancy and he had *trusted* her. Even when Melissa had probably told him the same thing when she had been deliberately trying to trap him into marriage. With that kind of history he would have been insane to trust her to that degree.

But he had. He still did. By the time either of them had the opportunity to buy condoms, it seemed as if it would be taking back that trust. Negating it.

The bubble of joy that Alice felt encased in these days was all the more astonishing because that level of trust—on both sides—and the fact that neither had sug-

gested any kind of a backward step, made it seem as if
they both knew they had found something permanent.

Sane people only had unprotected sex in a relationship where they felt safe. And safe meant commitment,
didn't it? An unspoken pact that it was going somewhere important.

They'd both been celibate for so long as well, which
implied that casual sex held no attraction for either of
them. To take this step was huge.

And the sex was...amazing. Incredible. Andrew
made her feel *so* beautiful. So desirable. So—

'Are you going to eat that last roll or just sit there
communicating telepathically with it?'

Alice laughed, blushed and reached for the last piece
of sushi. 'Sorry.'

'Don't be. It's great to see you so happy and being in
love turns anyone's brains to mush. It's a recognised medical condition, you know.' Jo was grinning. 'It's probably
just as well that you and Andy don't work the same shifts
too often. You gave yourselves away with the static that
radiates off both of you when you look at each other. It's
a wonder the department still functions properly.'

'Hey, we focus totally on our jobs when we're here.'

Jo gathered the empty containers to dump in the
rubbish bin. 'We make people turn off their cellphones
so it doesn't interfere with electronic equipment. I
reckon people in love should have to be separated. What
if you and Andy caught sight of each other on either side
of an IV pump? You could have some poor patient being
administered a lethal dose of insulin or something.'

Alice was laughing again as she followed Jo back
into the department. If anything, the silly conversation

was making her even happier. To generate such an obvious aura, the power had to be coming from both sides and that had to mean that Andrew felt the same way she did, even though he hadn't said anything.

It had to mean she wasn't wrong in dreaming of a future with this man. And with the little girl she was coming to love as much as any real mother could.

There was no real reason to drop into the emergency department on his way to pick Emmy up from school. Not on his day off. Well, he *had* left some journals in his office that he would love to catch up on but a text to Alice would have been enough to have her collect them on his behalf.

The house had felt empty all day, that was the problem. Walking over the hills with only Jake for company earlier this afternoon had felt wrong. The weight of that empty feeling in his gut had made him stop at the highest point on the route and gaze down at this amazing property he now owned.

He could see the beautiful old house with smoke curling from two of its chimneys. Funny how quickly he'd got used to living in such a vast space. It was time to start planning restoration work and finding enough furniture to make it all feel homely. The project was exciting but daunting. Hopefully, Alice would have an idea of where to start.

The old shearer's cottage looked tiny in comparison and deserted for the moment with no evidence of a fire and warmth within. Not far from the cottage was the paddock where Ben and Paddington were eating the supply of hay Alice must have fed out before leaving for work before dawn this morning.

The recognition of what that empty feeling inside was all about hit Andrew like a solid object. This place was all about Alice and she wasn't here with him. He needed her here because he was beginning to realise what an integral part Alice was of this whole picture.

Over the last few weeks they had all come to know each other so well. The adults, child and animals. Andrew could touch the top of Jake's head as he stood there, musing, and he loved the way the dog leaned in against his leg, the way he always did with Alice. He was part of Jake's clan now. Worthy of companionship and protection. Part of the family.

It made him catch his breath. Sure, Alice still slipped back to the cottage before Emmy woke in the mornings. They had agreed it was wise to keep up the charade of her occupying her own dwelling and bed but, to all intents and purposes, they were functioning as a family, albeit with two very busy parents who were keeping up full-time employment.

It wasn't a huge stretch of imagination to think of a future that was a little different. One where Alice might want to spend more of her time at home, maybe.

With the children.

He could imagine a toddler, safely strapped into a pushchair and parked in the corner of a paddock with Jake on guard nearby. They would be watching as Alice gave Emmy another one of her astonishingly patient riding lessons. His first born would be wearing the helmet she was so proud of it had to sit on her bedside table at night and her face would be set in those determined lines, like the ones he'd seen yesterday. Paddington had been going round in circles with Alice on the end of the lead rope and Emmy had been bouncing and bumping up and down in the saddle, trying very hard to learn to rise to the trot.

There'd be a high chair at the end of that table in the kitchen and there'd be lots of laughter as a meal was shared.

And then the children would be tucked up in bed and he and Alice would have the rest of the evening to themselves. To talk about their lives and work and children. To dream about the future and, finally, to go to their bed.

They knew each other so well that way now, too. They knew the intricate maps of each other's bodies. The places to touch or kiss or lick that would elicit a sigh of pleasure or a soft sound of escalating need. Andrew knew when to slow down to take Alice to the brink and then make it last until she was desperate for release. For the bone-softening satisfaction that *he* could give her.

He wanted her again, just thinking about it.

He wanted everything she was giving him. Them. And he wanted to erase the nebulous fear that it might not last. Was it too soon to talk about marriage? A commitment for life?

…love?

Yes. Judging by the way his heart rate picked up and his mouth went dry, the prospect was enough to make him afraid. Of what—that she might say no? That he might be wrong and it would be buying into the same kind of heartache he couldn't contemplate enduring again? Especially now, because he knew it would be far worse this time. He'd never felt this way about Melissa. Had never felt this odd emptiness because she wasn't by his side. He'd never once looked at her and imagined her being his wife and the mother of his children the way he had that night when Alice had knelt in front of his fire and offered to be Emmy's nanny.

The decision regarding Melissa's place in his life had been so easy to make. Simply a matter of doing the right thing. Was he hoping at some unconscious level that Alice would make another decision easy and make entertaining any doubts a waste of time and energy? That something would happen to push her more firmly into his arms, like...getting pregnant?

Was that why he'd been insane enough to contemplate having unprotected sex? No. Of course not. He'd never be that irresponsible. On the other hand, if it did happen—eventually—he would be thrilled. The million dollar question was how Alice would feel about it.

Time, Andrew decided on his way down the hill with Jake. He just needed more time to get used to this. To erase those last lingering doubts all by himself. He had to be sure, for Emmy's sake, and there was no rush, was there?

Alice didn't want to go anywhere else.

Something didn't feel right.

Alice couldn't put her finger on quite what it was, but she was feeling almost disconnected from what she was doing. The graph on the chart where she was recording the figures of a blood pressure she had just taken looked oddly fuzzy. And then her stomach rumbled so loudly the young man on the bed grinned broadly.

'Someone needs lunch,' he said.

Alice shook her head. 'I had a huge lunch not that long ago.'

Her stomach growled again and this time Alice felt it turn over and squeeze. She also experienced a very unpleasant wave of sensation that made her skin prickle.

'Excuse me,' she said to her patient.

She needed to go and get some fresh air. Or, better yet, splash a bit of cold water on her face.

She found Jo in the locker room toilets with her hand cupped under the cold tap, scooping water into her mouth.

'Jo! What's wrong? You look awful!'

Jo rinsed her mouth and spat. 'I feel awful. I've just been throwing up. Oh, God, I can't be pregnant.' She raised a very pale face to look at Alice. 'I just *can't* be!'

The mention of throwing up was doing something peculiar to Alice. A wave of nausea so powerful it made spots dance in front of her eyes took hold. She clamped a hand over her mouth and made a dive into one of the cubicles.

A very long minute later, she staggered to the basins to copy Jo's mouth-rinsing technique. Lifting her head with what felt like a supreme effort, she found Jo staring at her in the mirror with a grimace that was a creditable attempt at a smile.

'Hallelujah,' Jo groaned. 'It must have been the sushi!'

Poking his head around the curtain of Cubicle 6, where the busy triage nurse had informed him he would find Alice, the last thing Andrew had expected to find was that she was lying on the bed instead of tending to a patient.

'Good *grief*! What's wrong?' Concern hit him right in the gut. As hard as it might have if he'd found Emmy lying in a hospital bed.

Alice's lips were almost as pale as her face and it seemed to be an effort for her to move them.

'Food…poisoning.'

'Oh, no! Lunch?'

'Mmm.' Alice still hadn't opened her eyes. 'Me and Jo… Chicken…sushi.'

The mention of food appeared to be too much. Alice rolled onto her side with a groan and reached for a vomit container.

Andrew already had it in his hand. He supported her head with his free hand until she was finished and then helped her back onto the pillow. He picked up the damp towel clearly there for wiping her face.

'How long have you been like this?'

Alice managed a faint wry smile. 'Too long.' She tried to take the cloth from his hand but he kept wiping gently and she gave up, her hand flopping back onto the bed. 'I think I'm dying.'

'You'd better not be,' Andrew said mildly, trying to ignore the way her words made him ache to hold and comfort her. Trying even harder not to see the dreadful dark chasm that cracked open in the back of his mind at the thought. 'Emmy hasn't learned to trot properly yet.'

An attempt at laughter only made Alice throw up again.

'Sorry.' But he'd been able to make her laugh even when she was feeling so miserable. Curiously, that made him feel good. 'Poor you,' he added sympathetically. 'I think we'd better get you home, don't you?'

'No.' Alice rolled her head sideways. 'I'll just stay here and die quietly. I'd hate to be sick in your nice car.'

'Where's Jo?'

'Her flatmate came and took her home.'

'And that's exactly where I'm taking you. Home.' He might be taking advantage of the fact that Alice was in no condition to argue, but there was no way he wasn't going to win this round. 'I want you where I can look after you. Don't move, I'm going to go and get a wheel-chair.'

He obtained a pile of vomit containers and their lids as well. And lots of clean towels, which was a good thing because the movement of the car only made things worse. Not that Alice had anything left in her stomach to get rid of. Between bouts of nausea she rested her head back and kept her eyes firmly shut.

Emmy took one look at the closed eyes and pale face through the side window as Andrew led her to the car a short time later and she stopped in her tracks. Her bottom lip trembled.

'What's wrong with Alice?'

'She's feeling a bit sick. She ate some bad food for her lunch.'

His hand was being gripped as hard as a five-year-old was capable of gripping. He could sense the tension in her whole body as she continued staring. Alice still had her eyes closed so she was unaware of the horrified scrutiny.

Emmy's voice had a heartbreaking wobble. 'She's not going to die, is she, Daddy?'

Oh, no! Why hadn't it occurred to him that seeing Alice like this might be traumatic for a child who'd lost her mother?

'No, darling.' Andrew scooped her up. 'She just needs to be looked after for a bit. She'll be feeling much better by tomorrow.'

'But…she *might* die. Like my mummy did.'

'No.' Andrew pressed his lips against Emmy's hair. 'I told her she's not allowed to because you haven't learned to trot on Paddington Bear yet. Come on, we need to get home and then you can help me look after Alice. I'll be the doctor and you can be the nurse, okay?'

'And we'll make her better?'

'We sure will.'

'Are you really, really sure?'

'Yes.' Andrew put Emmy down and moved to open the back door of his car.

'That's good,' Emmy said. 'I don't want Alice to be sick.'

'Neither do I,' Andrew murmured, waiting for Emmy to climb inside so he could do up her seat belt. He took a deep breath, letting his gaze rest for a moment on the back of the auburn head close beside him.

'Neither do I,' he said again, surprising himself with the absolute conviction his words contained.

The worst was over within twenty-four hours but Alice felt about as energetic as a wet dish cloth.

Lying here, propped up on numerous pillows, with her dog beside the bed and a small girl tucked up against her body, Alice thought she might never want to move again.

'Are you *still* here, Em?' Andrew came into the room with a steaming mug on a saucer in his hand. 'You're supposed to be letting Alice rest, remember?'

'I *am*,' Emmy said indignantly. 'I'm just giving her cuddles.'

Alice smiled. 'Very nice cuddles they are, too.'

'Are they helping you get better?'

'Definitely. I haven't been sick for hours and hours now.'

'You'll be dehydrated.' Alice felt the bed dip as Andrew sat down on the edge, reaching to put the mug on the bedside table. 'I thought you might be getting sick of flat lemonade.'

'It *smells* nice,' Alice said cautiously.

'It's tomato.' Andrew smiled. 'I know you're supposed to tempt convalescents with chicken soup, but it's not exactly the flavour of the month around here, is it?'

'No.' For a moment, Alice let herself bask in the knowledge that Andrew had thought of bringing soup at all. That he wanted to care for her. She could feel the firmness of his thigh pressing against hers and the bedclothes might as well have not been there.

Emmy was curled up on her other side and Jake had his head up, sniffing the air and eyeing the slivers of dry toast decorating the saucer that held the mug of soup.

When was the last time Alice had felt nurtured like this? Surrounded by…family.

Not since she was a child and there'd just been herself and her grandmother back then. This felt like a real family. Complete.

She would never find anything else quite like this. No one that she wanted to be with as much as this man and child. It was enough to bring a painful lump to her throat.

'Want to try the soup?' Andrew asked hopefully.

'In a bit.' Alice's voice had a telltale wobble.

Emmy levered herself up instantly. Well practised now in her role as a nurse, she laid a small hand on Alice's forehead. She frowned.

'I think you have a t-tremp—'

'Temperature?' Andrew supplied. He lifted his hand and replaced Emmy's. 'No. It feels just fine to me.'

The touch was soft. He stroked it upwards to smooth unbrushed curls away and the gesture was a caress. One that matched the softness in his eyes as he held Alice's gaze.

Emmy was watching. 'Maybe Alice should go in *your* bed, Daddy.'

'Oh?' Alice could see the way Andrew's pupils dilated a fraction. Desire? Or alarm? 'Why do you say that, sweetheart?'

'Because that's where I go when I feel sick and it always makes me feel better.'

'Oh…' Andrew smiled into Alice's eyes. 'Would it make *you* feel better, do you think, Alice?'

'Um…perhaps not right now.' There was a bubble of laughter growing now. A silent communication that was a shared joy. She was sure she could see a reflection of what she was feeling.

A love so strong it was overwhelming.

'No.' Andrew was nodding gravely. 'Not right now. It's soup time for you. And you, young lady…' He rolled so that he was eye to eye with his daughter over the slope of Alice's hip. 'You need to come with me. We've got one horse and one pony that need some hay.'

The effects of the food poisoning were hard to shake off.

It was several days before Alice felt well enough to

go back to work. That it might take a lot longer to share Andrew's bed again was a disturbing prospect.

'I missed a pill,' she confessed after a long tender kiss as they sat on the couch together late at night. 'Two, in fact.'

'There wouldn't have been much point in taking them when you couldn't keep anything down, anyway.' Andrew's hand traced her ribs and rested on the jut of her hip bone. 'You've lost weight, love. Are you sure you're feeling up to this?'

'I'm fine but…it's too risky.'

'I have a good supply of condoms,' Andrew told her. 'I bought them weeks ago after that first night.'

'You did?' Alice's eyes widened. 'You never mentioned that.'

'Didn't see the need. It's extra protection now, though, if you want the insurance.'

If she wanted it? What was Andrew suggesting—that it wouldn't be a disaster if she got pregnant?

Yes, it would.

Pregnancy had been the way Melissa had trapped Andrew. Blackmailed him into marriage. It was the absolute last thing Alice would want to have happen.

Especially now, when everything seemed to be going in the direction she'd dreamed of. When it seemed more than likely that Andrew would propose to her.

When he was ready. He had to know, as definitively as Alice did, that he wanted them to be together for the rest of their lives. She was quite prepared to wait for as long as that might take.

She didn't have any intention of going anywhere else.

* * *

Jo bounced back from the sushi incident far more quickly than Alice.

'Great way to lose a couple of kilos,' she said a week later.

'Are you kidding? I'd rather hit the gym every day for a month than go through that.'

'You don't look like you're in any state to go near a gym. Are you okay?'

'I've felt better. It's taking a while to feel like eating properly again, that's all.'

The first alarm bells rang the following week when Alice still felt unwell every time she looked at food.

When she realised she was now several days late for her period.

It was easy enough to find a pregnancy test kit in the emergency department and take it into the locker room toilets when she had a quiet moment.

Far harder to try and deal with the shocking result.

She *was* pregnant.

So much for the extra insurance. They'd made love the night before she'd become ill and that had been in the middle of her cycle. The timing couldn't have been worse. Just a few days either side and it wouldn't have mattered that her chemical protection had been disrupted.

Alice sat on the closed lid of the toilet and buried her face in her hands.

She had to face the fact that it had happened.

And that she was now going to have to try and find a way to tell Andrew. To tell him that history was repeating itself. To give him reason to think that she might be no better than Melissa and trying to force him into marriage. *She* had taken responsibility for contraception. *He* had trusted her and she had broken that trust.

It didn't matter how tightly pressed her hands were against her eyes. The tears still seeped through.

CHAPTER EIGHT

DENIAL was a wonderful thing.

Alice knew perfectly well it was only a temporary refuge but it was impossible to resist. Her reasoning was along the kind of lines that had stopped her pushing Andrew to talk about his time with Melissa and what his marriage had been like.

She didn't want to know because, deep down, she was afraid it might tarnish the glow of what they had found in this new life together. And what she had to tell him now would inevitably do the same thing and that meant she would never again get as close as she was at this moment to living her dream. Who could blame her if she wanted to delay the falling of the axe for just a few days?

Enough time to soak in memories to treasure.

The way Andrew smiled at her. That careless touch as he passed sometimes. Just a brush of her hand or touch on her arm or even simply a meaningful glance if they were at work. If she was busy in the kitchen at home, and Emmy wasn't close by, he might lift her hair to drop a kiss on her neck or put his arms around her waist and draw her back so that her rump was nestled in his groin for a second or two.

Even more intimately, there was that look in his eyes just before he kissed her properly. When they lay with their heads on the pillows of Andrew's bed, their faces so close it was hard to focus. That was what Alice was going to miss the most. The feel, more than the look, of being trusted.

Being loved.

For a few days it worked wonderfully well. Increasingly, however, Alice could feel the claws of guilt digging in. She had wanted to win Andrew's trust so much and here she was keeping a secret he had every right to know.

Work was a blessing because it was so much easier to push anything personal so far into the background it could be virtually forgotten. Until she had to deal with a case that hit a little too close to home.

Laura Green was a thirty-two-year-old woman who had presented with sudden onset vaginal bleeding and she was terrified that she was miscarrying. Her husband, John, was with her and, while he was doing a great job of support and reassurance, Alice could see the same fear in his eyes.

'It's okay, babe. Don't cry.'

But Laura was sobbing as she climbed onto the bed and Alice helped her out of her clothes and into a gown. She could empathise with this woman's fear.

Losing her own baby was already unthinkable. It was a part of her. A part of the man she loved. Inside her belly and growing stronger every day.

While the consequences of revealing her secret were

terrifying, there were moments when Alice couldn't help being thrilled. No matter how things worked out between herself and Andrew, she wanted this baby very, very much. She would love it and protect it and care for it.

As a solo mother?

It was unfortunate that the doctor assigned to Laura's case chose that precise moment to enter the cubicle. Even more so that it happened to be Andrew. Thankfully, Alice was busy shoving her patient's personal property into a large paper bag. The rustle of the paper covered her sharp intake of breath and she had a moment, as she bent to push the bag into the basket under the bed, when she could blink really hard and ensure that the threat of tears was banished.

This was one of those chin-raising moments.

If she had to be a solo mother then she would cope. It was a long way from how she would want things to be, but she'd been dealing with that kind of disappointment her whole life, hadn't she? Chasing dreams and then making the best of what was left when the dream evaporated.

And she'd had the feeling all along that what she'd found with Andrew and Emmy was too good to last for ever. She was prepared. Or she would be, very soon.

'How many weeks pregnant are you, Laura?' Andrew was asking.

'Almost ten.'

'And you've had a scan to confirm the pregnancy?'

'Last week.' Laura's voice broke. 'We…we saw the heart beating and…and they said that everything looked…fine.'

'Is this your first pregnancy?'

Laura couldn't answer. She had pressed her face against her husband's chest and he was holding her as her shoulders heaved with silent sobs.

'We've been trying for ages,' John said. 'And…yes, this is the first pregnancy.'

'Any abdominal pain?'

'No.' Laura raised a tear-streaked face. 'Am I going to lose my baby?'

'We'll have an answer to that soon,' Andrew told her gently. 'I'm going to examine you to see whether your cervix is open or closed and, depending on what I find, we'll look at doing an ultrasound test as well. Alice, could you get a blood pressure for me, please?'

'Sure.' It was good to have something to do instead of standing there with her thoughts spinning in ever decreasing circles.

She really hoped that Laura wasn't losing this baby, but the first twelve weeks was when the majority of miscarriages occurred.

How long had Melissa waited to break the news of her pregnancy to Andrew? Had she told him very early before she entered this higher risk period for miscarriage so she could be sure of securing the marriage proposal she desired? Or had she waited out the first trimester to get past a time that many people might consider a termination to be acceptable?

Maybe Alice would be damned either way—too soon or too late.

She wrapped the blood pressure cuff around Laura's upper arm. This was important because, if a miscarriage was underway, Laura's blood pressure could be dropping to dangerously low levels. She picked up the bulb of the sphygmomanometer and started squeezing it.

'This will get tight on your arm for a bit,' she warned.

The pressure inside Alice's head seemed to increase as she watched the mercury level rise. With the stethoscope in her ears, she could hear the rapid pounding of her own heart.

She wasn't anything like Melissa but would Andrew see that?

He still never mentioned his dead wife. Alice had been only too happy to sidestep the issue. To go along with the pretence that Melissa had never existed and therefore didn't matter.

How wrong had she been? Their marriage and the reason for it couldn't matter more now. History repeating itself. It was...huge and dark and very scary.

'Blood pressure's 130 over 85,' she reported.

'Is that good?' John asked anxiously.

'Probably up a little,' Andrew responded calmly. 'Only to be expected given the stress level.' He was pulling on some gloves. 'Tell me about this bleeding.'

'It was so sudden,' Laura said in a horrified kind of whisper. 'I was just standing there and all of a sudden I felt this trickle down my legs and I looked down and saw it was blood and—' Her words trailed into silence.

'She screamed,' John added in a hollow voice. 'I knew something awful had happened. I just picked her up and ran to the car. I didn't even think to call an ambulance or anything.'

'Did the bleeding continue at that rate?'

'No. I had a towel to sit on in the car but there

wasn't much on it by the time we got here. Is…is that good?' Laura sounded more than hopeful now. She sounded desperate.

'Let's have a look.' Andrew made sure the curtains around the cubicle were closed and then drew the sheet back. 'Bend your legs up for me, Laura.'

The examination took only a minute. Andrew's gloves were bloodstained as he pulled them off but his words were as good as could be hoped for.

'Your cervix is still tightly closed,' he told Laura.

'That's good, isn't it?'

'It's not a definitive answer yet but if it was open we'd have to say that yes, you were having a miscarriage.'

'What happens now?' John asked.

'We'll do an ultrasound to check for a foetal heartbeat. If we find one, it will be good news and all we'll need to do is keep Laura under observation for an hour or two to make sure that the bleeding has settled. We'll run some blood tests, too and monitor temperature and things just to rule out any kind of infection being the cause for this.'

Nobody asked about what would happen if they didn't find that heartbeat. The ramifications of that were only too obvious.

It was Andrew who did the ultrasound examination a short time later. John and Laura were holding hands tightly and Alice stood on the other side of the bed. Andrew had a hip on the bed with one hand holding the transducer to position it on Laura's still flat belly. With his other hand, he was pointing to part of the image on the screen which he had angled to allow the young couple to watch.

'That's the bladder,' he said, indicating a darker blob. 'And this is…' he changed the angle of the transducer '…the uterus.'

It felt as if everybody in this space was holding their breath. There were dozens of other patients in this department at the moment and a hive of activity beyond the flimsy fabric of the curtains, but Alice knew she wasn't the only one totally oblivious to anything other than that screen. She watched Andrew press the transducer down a little more firmly. She saw the tiny furrow between his brows.

And then, there it was. A rhythmic movement on the screen. A pulse of life.

Laura gasped and then twisted her face to look up at her husband. The relief and then the hope radiating from both their faces was blinding. Alice had to look away and she found her gaze caught by Andrew.

The look she was receiving was so soft. So warm. He wanted to share the joy of these young parents.

It was too much. The threat of tears so overwhelming that Alice had to look away instantly.

'Excuse me,' she whispered. 'I have to—'

To escape.

She turned and all but ran from the cubicle.

Alice had just bustled past Andrew without looking in his direction.

She was obviously busy, with a sealed bag of blood samples in her hands, but this was the second, or was it the third time, she'd missed the opportunity for eye contact on this shift.

And that was weird.

Almost as if she was avoiding him.

Andrew's frown deepened as he turned back to the X-ray image on the computer in front of him.

'That bad?' Peter stopped to peer over Andrew's shoulder.

'Not at all. Straightforward undisplaced radial fracture. Nothing a short stint in a cast won't make as good as new.'

Peter nodded. 'You must have been thinking about something else, then, to make you look so worried.'

'Was I looking worried?' Andrew tried to sound nonchalant.

'Yep.' The head of department raised an eyebrow. 'You're sure there's nothing I can help with?'

'I'm good,' Andrew said firmly. He smiled to prove it.

'No hassles getting properly settled, then? You're happy you made such a big move?'

'Oh, yes.' From the corner of his eye he could see Alice on her return journey from wherever she'd been taking the blood samples. 'Couldn't be happier.' Andrew felt his smile broadening and couldn't help glancing away from his colleague.

Peter followed his line of sight. 'Ahh...' The murmur was both understanding and approving.

'Hey!' Andrew's call was soft but Alice looked up.

She smiled brightly. Too brightly?

'Everything all right?'

'Of course.' The answer was quick. Alice was looking startled, as if it had been an odd thing for him to ask.

'How's Laura doing?'

'Fine. Bleeding's still minimal so she'll be able to go home very soon.'

Alice had noticed Peter standing behind Andrew now. She looked at the departmental head and then her gaze shifted back to Andrew before sliding away. She *was* avoiding eye contact. Why? Because Peter was there? Surely she realised that everybody knew about their relationship by now so why did she seem…what… nervous?

'I'd better get on with…' The rest of Alice's words were lost, partly because she was muttering but more because she was already moving swiftly away from the two men.

Andrew flicked a glance up at Peter but he was staring after Alice with a rather thoughtful expression. As though he'd noticed something a bit different about her as well.

'I'll leave you to it,' was all he said to Andrew. 'I've got some paperwork I should catch up on while things are quiet. Don't forget that senior staff meeting at shift changeover. The more that can make it the better.'

Andrew's hand curled over the computer mouse, clicking through images to make sure he hadn't missed anything.

He felt as if he was missing something but he knew it had nothing to do with the patient who'd fractured his arm. It had something to do with Alice. With why she'd been distant ever since…

Since they'd worked together earlier to assess Laura with her threatened miscarriage. Since that moment of relief when he'd located the heartbeat on ultrasound and could pretty much guarantee that the young couple weren't going to lose their baby.

Amidst the pleasure of a good outcome for their patient, Andrew had been acutely aware of a much more personal reaction to the scene. An odd flash of longing. He'd spared just a moment to wish that it was Alice on a bed having undergone an ultrasound examination and that he was holding her hand and they were both celebrating the proof that they were expecting a new addition to their family.

Had he somehow communicated something of that longing?

Good grief! If the idea of having a baby of their own was enough to scare Alice off he'd better rethink the whole idea of proposing marriage. Maybe she wasn't ready for that kind of commitment.

Maybe all she'd wanted all along was the guarantee of continuing to live in the place she loved.

No. Andrew actually physically shook his head as he pushed his chair back and stood up, ready to go back to his patient and arrange transfer to the plaster room.

Alice wasn't like that. She'd never use someone to get what she wanted. Deceive them emotionally.

She wasn't anything like Melissa had been.

He couldn't possibly be that wrong about the woman he was in love with. Any doubts he might have had regarding the strength of his feelings towards Alice had been well and truly dispelled during that food poisoning episode. Apart from Emmy, there was no one he cared about this much. Or ever would.

He'd been waiting for Alice to recover completely so that they could enjoy a real celebration. Waiting for the right moment to tell her how he felt and what he was dreaming of for their future.

Clearly, the right moment was not going to be anytime very soon.

Later that afternoon that moment seemed to recede even further.

A skeleton staff had been left in the department for the few minutes when senior doctors and nurses gathered in the staff room. Andrew came in last, having given Laura the all-clear to go home and stop worrying. He scanned the crowded staff room from where he had to stand close to the door, looking for Alice, unsure of whether she was here or not.

He wanted to catch her before she left to collect Emmy from school because he wanted to suggest that he bring takeaway food home for dinner tonight and make things easier for Alice. She still looked a bit peaky even though she should be well over the knock of being so ill for a couple of days.

'I didn't want to send out a general memo,' Peter told the group, 'and I'd appreciate it if what's being said stays in this room, but you're all here because you have keys to the drugs cabinet and I need you all to know there's been some anomalies noted recently in drug tallies.'

There she was—at the back of the room, sitting beside Jo.

It took Andrew a moment to register and then comprehend the strange look Alice was giving him. Her chin was up and she looked defensive. Cold, even.

Oh...Lord! Did she think he'd been seeking her out because of the mention of an issue regarding restricted drugs?

Was it possible that she still believed he had any doubts about her trustworthiness?

Peter was saying something about records needing to be meticulous. About the work he was having to do to try and go through patient notes and match the drugs administered with what had been recorded as being taken from the locked cabinet. Andrew wasn't listening.

He'd left it too long to say something to Alice, hadn't he? With the best of intentions, Andrew had tried to prove his trust in another way, but in that tiny moment of eye contact across the crowded staff room he knew, without a shadow of doubt, that he'd been wrong.

That he was in trouble.

For the first time since they'd got into the routine of this shared care for Emmy, Alice didn't stay to eat the dinner she'd prepared.

'I've got too much to catch up on,' she'd excused herself the moment Andrew came through the door. 'Washing and emails and…you know…domestic stuff.'

And she'd fled, without giving him time to say anything. The way she had after that staff meeting this afternoon. Alice really did need some time to herself. In her little cottage, with Jake for company and a lovely, deep hot bath to soak in.

Time to try and deal with the fact that, after so many blissful weeks, her life was unravelling yet again. Totally. At home and at work, which made this the most difficult crisis she had ever had to face.

Was somebody really stealing drugs in their department? Maybe it would turn out to be a storm in a teacup and someone had just been slack about doing the paperwork. It certainly wasn't her. Ever since her time in London, Alice had been paranoid about the regulations to do with handling restricted drugs. She checked and double-checked absolutely everything and always got someone else to repeat the checks and sign off what she'd done.

She'd still been the first person Andrew had looked at, though, hadn't she?

The mud was still sticking and no amount of soaking in comforting, hot baths was going to wash it out of her life. Just a flicker of suspicion was all it took. Alice was never going to escape the past.

Neither was Andrew, although he didn't realise it yet. He'd know soon enough when Alice confessed and she had to tell him soon because any window of justifying denial was definitely over.

Tomorrow, she decided. She'd tell him tomorrow.

But Alice was working the following day and Andrew had a day off. He took Emmy to a movie in the afternoon and they stayed in town for dinner. Then Alice had an early start and Andrew had a shift that started mid-afternoon and went through till midnight.

She slept in the spare room that night. The one she'd used when they'd first put this plan into action. The bed felt cold and unused. It hadn't been used since she and Andrew had started sharing *his* bed. Alice heard him come in in the early hours of the morning. She heard him call her name very softly from the door.

She pretended to be soundly asleep, hoping that Andrew would come in anyway and get into *her* bed and hold her. Maybe then she could tell him and maybe—just maybe—they could work through it.

Andrew stood there for a long moment. And then she

heard his steps on the wooden floorboards as he made his way to his own room.

The longer she waited, the more nervous Alice became. So nervous that when she and Andrew were working the same shift together a couple of days later, she could barely concentrate on her work.

She dropped things. She bumped into a trolley and sent supplies crashing to the floor. She felt ridiculously close to tears for most of the day. It was no great surprise when Peter quietly asked her to come and see him in his office. Alice knew that Andrew was watching her walk away with the head of department but she couldn't look back. She didn't want to be given sympathy or reassurance she really didn't deserve.

Peter didn't waste any time coming to the point.

'What on earth's wrong today, Alice? You're not yourself at all.'

Alice couldn't deny the accusation. 'I...I'm sorry, Peter.'

'Are you sick?'

She shook her head. 'I've just got...something on my mind.'

'Hmm. I had that impression quite a few days ago. You've been...I don't know...kind of edgy.'

'Sorry. I'll get it sorted.'

'Anything I can do to help?'

Alice shook her head again. 'It's got nothing to do with work.'

'Are you sure?'

Alice blinked. Was he asking her whether this had something to do with her relationship with one of his consultants? Did everybody know about her and Andrew now? She couldn't tell him, though. Not before she'd told Andrew.

'It doesn't have anything to do with the issue we've got with missing drugs, does it?'

Alice sucked in her breath. 'What do you mean?'

Peter sighed. 'I know about London, Alice. About why you had to resign from the job you had there.'

Alice gaped at him. 'Who told you about that?'

There was only one possible suspect she could think of and that was so painful she wanted to curl up and die. The ultimate betrayal. She didn't want to know but she had to.

'Was it Andrew Barrett?'

'No.'

It wasn't Peter who answered the question. Alice jerked her head around to find Andrew standing in the doorway of the office. He stepped inside. 'I most certainly didn't say anything. In fact, I'm as interested as you are to find out who did.'

They both looked at Peter who looked away from Alice to Andrew. 'You replaced Dave when you took on your position here.'

'That's correct.'

'You worked with him years ago, yes?'

'Also correct. I don't really see what this has to do with Alice.'

Peter's tone was bland. He was delivering facts here, not an opinion. 'He made some enquiries from mutual associates before he approached you. He spoke to quite a few people and they invariably recommended you very highly. One doctor told him about the New Zealand nurse who'd come under suspicion for stealing drugs. Told him how well you'd dealt with a potentially damaging situation in your department. Dave felt obliged to pass the information on to me when he learned that the nurse spoken about was back working here again.'

'You never said anything to me,' Alice said quietly. 'Why not?'

'You've never done anything to make me think there was anything I needed to say.'

'Until now? Until drugs started to go missing?'

'Until now,' Peter agreed. 'When something's obviously upsetting you so much you're unable to do your job with the kind of competency I've come to rely on.'

'Alice had nothing to do with the drugs in London going missing.'

Andrew spoke with such conviction that both Alice and Peter stared at him.

'You sound like you found out who did,' Peter said.

'I did. And it wasn't Alice.'

'Who was it?' The query came from Peter but he was voicing what was filling her mind, along with so much else she couldn't collect the words, let alone say them.

He'd *known*? She'd thought he'd given her the gift of trust but he'd never had a reason to *mis*trust her. It had been an empty gift.

A sham.

Andrew hadn't answered Peter's query because at that same moment, his pager had gone off with a strident alarm that signalled an urgent call. He glanced down to where it was clipped to his belt, turning it enough to read the display.

'Arrest,' he snapped. 'Resus 1.'

Peter was going to accompany him. Both men were moving fast.

'Who was it?' Alice had to ask as they passed. 'Who *did* take those drugs, Andrew?'

He spared her only a graze of eye contact.

'Melissa.'

CHAPTER NINE

SHOCK gave way to anger.

No. Make that cold fury.

All this time, Alice had been so grateful to be given a chance to prove herself. To win Andrew's trust, despite any reason he might have had for doubting her.

And he'd never had that reason. He'd *known* she was innocent. He could have cleared her name years and years ago and saved her the haunting aftermath of that shameful incident. In fact, hadn't she handed him the perfect opportunity to do exactly that?

You still believe I took those drugs, don't you?

He could have told her then. He *should* have told her then. Instead, he'd simply denied ever saying it. And when she'd reminded him that he'd said he couldn't trust her, she could see that the statement still held truth. That was why she had set out to prove herself.

He'd lied to her. By omission maybe, but that didn't make it any more forgivable.

Especially when she had trusted *him* so absolutely, even though she was aware he was keeping an important part of his life a secret. His whole marriage. Emmy's infancy. She'd colluded in sweeping it under the mat but there was no way she would have done that if she'd known how huge that secret was. Or that it directly affected *her*. She'd had a right to that information. As much as Andrew had a right to know she was carrying his baby.

Oh...God! What a mess!

The bottom line was that Andrew hadn't trusted her. For whatever reason—and, whatever it was, it wouldn't be good enough—he'd lied to her.

And she'd really believed that there was a future for them?

Talk about being blinded by love.

Right now, her vision was clouded more by fury and the pain of betrayal.

Having paced Peter's office for goodness knew how long, with her arms wrapped tightly around her body, her head spinning and the pain of grief already closing a vice-like grip around her heart, Alice finally let go of herself, lifted her chin, gritted her teeth and moved.

The cardiac arrest scenario in Resus 1 was obviously not going very well. Through curtains that hadn't been fully closed, Alice could see the flat line running across the monitor where ECG spikes should have been. She could see the crowd of staff around the bed. Jo was doing chest compressions. A registrar stood to one side holding a bag-mask unit and another was drawing up fresh drugs. Andrew, grim-faced, was in the process of intubating what looked to be a fairly young man.

He would be doing everything he possibly could to save that life but Alice didn't have room in her heart to applaud his skill or dedication. If she went down that track she might start trying to understand why he'd betrayed her. To make excuses for him because she so desperately wanted this not to be ending.

But it was. It had to. She couldn't stay with a man she couldn't trust. A man who didn't trust her. She had to deal with it and move on.

Another nurse was recording everything that was happening in the resuscitation effort and yet more staff stood close by. Ready to assist if needed but, for the moment, there was nothing they could do. Peter was one of those extras and he was standing right beside the gap in the curtains. Alice went up to him.

'I'm sorry,' she said quietly. 'I know I haven't been doing my job properly but I'm going to sort it out, I promise.'

'Good.' But Peter was frowning in concern. 'Maybe you should take the rest of today off. I'll get cover arranged.'

'Thank you. I'd appreciate that.' Alice took a shaky inward breath. She could start that sorting out process immediately. 'Could you also please tell Dr Barrett that he'll have to make other arrangements to have his daughter collected from school. I won't be available.'

Peter was still frowning but there was surprise on his face as well. He could see there was more to this than he'd realised. 'Are you all right, Alice? Where are you going to be?'

'I'm fine. Or I will be. I'm going home. I have some urgent business to take care of.' Alice turned away to head for the locker room to collect her things. Urgent was the word for it, all right. How soon could she hope to find somewhere for Ben to go? That had to be the first priority. In a worst case scenario, she and Jake could survive in the truck for a few days but she couldn't abandon her horse.

Could she abandon Emmy?

Andrew?

She *had* to. Before her heart recovered enough to start fighting her head. Before it found a way to make what he'd done somehow acceptable. It wasn't and it never could be. She had to leave as quickly as she could manage and then get as far away as she possibly could.

Was she being a coward?

Yes, but there was only so much pain a person could front up for, wasn't there? Emmy and Andrew had each other. Alice had only herself to look to for protection now.

The resuscitation just went on and on.

Drug therapy produced a shockable rhythm. Defibrillation produced a normal-looking rhythm but, within a minute or two, no matter what they did, it degenerated back to a flat line.

Again and again, they shocked the heart but after nearly an hour they all knew that, even if they could get a rhythm capable of sustaining life, they would be saving someone who would be irreparably brain damaged from too long a period without a normal level of circulating oxygen.

'Time of death,' Andrew finally said in a tone resonant with defeat, 'Fourteen-oh-seven.'

The man had been only forty-four. A health fanatic who'd gone out for a run in his lunch break only to collapse in an isolated park corner where it had taken passers-by too long to see him. He wasn't that much older than Andrew, and that made it even harder to try and explain what had happened to his distraught wife and young children.

Having dealt with that gruelling interview, Andrew found Peter waiting for him with a message from Alice to say that he'd have to collect Emmy himself.

She wasn't available. What the hell did that mean?

'I'd better ring the school,' he said. 'I'll arrange care for her until I finish at six.'

'You could go early,' Peter suggested. 'I'm happy to cover for you.'

'Did Alice say *why* she was leaving so early?'

'She just said she had something urgent she needed to take care of at home.' Peter's gaze was very direct. 'I must say, I've never seen her looking quite that upset.'

Of course she was upset. By telling her that it was Melissa who'd stolen those drugs, Andrew had opened a can of worms he'd wanted so much to keep tightly closed.

What if Alice thought he'd known all along? That he'd been protecting his girlfriend and leaving her to take the blame.

At least he could put her straight on that score.

'I might just take you up on that offer to get away early,' he told Peter.

If he rang the school, he could arrange the care for Emmy anyway and then he could go home alone. He could find Alice and see how much of the damage—if any—he could repair.

Peter was nodding. 'When you see her,' he said, 'please apologise on my behalf for any insinuation I made. Someone came forward after that staff meeting the other day and told me about a messy time on a night shift recently. Multi-victim MVA and they were very short-staffed. I had someone looking into it and they've just told me that a total of seven ampoules of morphine were used that night and the nurse who had the key on that shift totally forgot to go back and sign them off in the cabinet logbook. The matter is closed as far as we're concerned.'

It wouldn't be for Alice, though, would it?

A short time later, with a face that was as grim as when he'd been trying to save the life of that heart attack victim, Andrew left the building.

Fear snapped at his heels. Or wheels. Thank heaven for his car's turn of speed and fabulous road-handling ability.

Putting himself in Alice's place, Andrew wouldn't be surprised to get to his property and find she'd packed up her things and left. He couldn't let that happen. He needed Alice in his life. So did Emmy.

He *loved* her and so did Emmy. He had to fight for both of them. For *all* of them, because they were a family.

Andrew didn't drive to his own house, he took the turn to the cottage and, thank God, her truck was there. Once on foot, it wasn't hard to locate Alice. She was in Ben's paddock, brushing him. Jake sat by the fence but he didn't move to greet Andrew and Alice didn't look up from what she was doing. Fear snapped again and managed to catch hold of his heart.

'Please, Alice. Stop what you're doing and talk to me.'

He got no response. Just a feeling of tension in the air that was a solid barrier. 'At least *look* at me.'

But Alice kept brushing the damn horse. Ben was tied up near the water trough. Almost the exact spot both he and Alice had been that day he'd arrived home to discover that she was his tenant. A saddle hung over the fence behind the trough and Alice was bent over, brushing mud from Ben's legs.

'Alice.'

'I can't stop,' she said. 'I've got an awful lot to get done.'

'Oh?' Did she have no idea how important it was for them to talk? Andrew felt as if he was being dismissed. That *they* were being dismissed. She couldn't be doing that so easily. That would make him wrong about so many things and he knew he wasn't that wrong. 'You can't be that busy if you're planning to go riding.'

Alice straightened at that and turned around. Andrew was shocked by the pain he could see in her eyes. It burned into him and he could *feel* it as his own pain.

'I'm riding Ben to his new paddock,' she said tonelessly. 'That way, I've got the horse float free to pack my stuff into.'

'Pack? You're *leaving*?' Even though the possibility had occurred to him, he hadn't really believed it. Or maybe he just hadn't known how hard it would hit him.

'Yes.'

Such a tiny word to have such enormous repercussions. Unacceptable repercussions.

'You can't leave! I won't let you.'

'You can't stop me.'

Andrew opened his mouth but then closed it again. What could he say? He knew Alice was upset. He could understand her being angry but to be walking out on him? On Emmy? He felt as though an enormous chasm was opening beneath his feet. He was in danger of falling and he couldn't think of how to prevent it. Or how to stop Alice. She was right. He couldn't stop her if she was as determined as she sounded. Not physically.

Alice had turned away again. She was reaching up to brush Ben's neck. 'We had a lucky break,' she said. 'When I was driving home I saw this woman out on the road, shifting her goat. I stopped and asked if she knew of anyone who might have some grazing available.'

Andrew heard the wobble in her voice and it felt as if a piece of his heart were being torn away.

Alice was hurting. Badly.

'It's not too far,' Alice continued doggedly. 'We can follow the river and cut across to the farm and...and Jake needs a good run.'

Jake looked as though he was as aware as Andrew of how Alice was feeling. The dog sat beside the trough, watching his mistress intently. Was he waiting for the chance to get close and offer comfort?

Someone had to.

'Alice, please. Let me explain.'

'No need,' she said hurriedly. She was brushing harder on what looked like a perfectly clean area of horse. 'I've put Paddington into the paddock closer to your house. He's got plenty of hay but he'll need some more in the morning.'

She stepped away from Ben, then moved towards the fence where she dropped the brush and reached for the saddle. Andrew moved as well. Close enough to reach out and catch her wrist.

'Listen to me,' he said urgently. 'I know what you're thinking, but I had no idea that Melissa was taking drugs when the trouble started in the department.'

Alice pulled her wrist free. She rubbed it, not looking at Andrew, and that seemed unfair. He knew he hadn't been holding her tightly enough to hurt. He would never deliberately hurt her in any way and that was making this unbearable. Something already tight inside him was stretching further. Getting ready to snap. He watched her pull her saddle off the fence and put it on Ben's back and didn't try to touch her again to stop her.

'When I did find out, I tried to tell you,' he said. 'I went to your address, only to find it empty. With a 'Sold' sign outside. Nobody knew where you'd gone. I was too late and I'm sorry.'

'It took *months* to sell that place,' Alice snapped. 'Months and months where I couldn't get another job or pay my mortgage. It was the bank who put it up for auction and sold it for as much as they needed to cover their debt. I lost everything I'd worked so hard for.'

'I know. I'm sorry, Alice. I can't tell you how sorry I am but I *didn't* know in time, I swear it.'

The huff of expelled breath was disparaging and Andrew's heart sank even further. A dead weight in his chest that was going to pull him into that chasm.

'Would you like to know when I did find out the truth?'

Yes. Of course she wanted to know.

No. She didn't want to hear him say anything more.

Just the sound of his voice was too much. The pain she could hear in it. The sincerity of his apology. Saying sorry couldn't undo the hurt. Or repair the lack of trust.

She kept her head bent, focusing on doing up girth buckles. She made no verbal response but Andrew kept talking anyway, after a pause that had only been long enough for him to draw a breath.

'The day Emmy was born,' he told her. 'When I found I had a baby who was in trouble because of the morphine she'd been exposed to during the pregnancy. When I had to stand back and watch my precious newborn child go through all the agony of drug withdrawal.'

Alice's head jerked up, her eyes wide with shock. It would be a horrific start to life for any baby but this was *Emmy* he was talking about. The little girl she loved dearly. The brave, determined child who was trying so hard to learn to trot on her fat little pony.

'She promised she'd go into rehab. That she would do whatever it took to be a good mother. A good *wife*.' Andrew couldn't help the bitter edge to that last word. 'But you know what she was really good at? Deception. When she wasn't working in the hospital any more she had to find new ways to feed her addictions. And when alcohol wasn't enough she took money I knew nothing about. She found sources for things like cocaine and even heroin in the end. She was so good at covering up her habit that I had to go home more than once and find my child totally neglected to face what was going on.'

The words were tumbling from Andrew in a wash of anger and sadness. Was that why he'd avoided ever talking about it? Because when he took the stopper out there was so much bottled up that he couldn't control it?

'Time after time I sent her off to rehab. Private, discreet clinics. Emmy didn't even recognise her when she came home sometimes. I had to cope with my job and raising my baby and keeping everything a secret and it nearly killed me.'

'Why?' Alice didn't understand. 'Why did it have to be a secret?' Especially now, so long after any danger to Emmy was over. Why did it have to have been a secret from *her*? 'Surely other people knew?'

'Only those involved in her treatment.' Andrew shook his head. 'Mel was an expert in manipulation. She could persuade anyone to fall into line if she was desperate enough. And if charm and sex didn't work, then blackmail was always an option. She threatened to take Emmy away and make sure I never got to see her again. I began to take more and more time off work to make sure she was safe. That they were both safe because I felt responsible. I was Emmy's father. Melissa's husband. There had to be some way I could get the hell that my life had become sorted out.'

Alice closed her eyes for a moment. This was all so horrible but she had to hear it all. 'And the accident?'

'She was loaded up to her eyeballs with prescription drugs that time. Washed down with alcohol. I'd taken Emmy to the park and came home to find Mel in a crumpled heap at the bottom of the stairs. I couldn't prove I hadn't been in the house at the time and I didn't want the details to come out. I was ashamed of myself. The way I'd handled things.'

There was no denying he'd handled things badly. Alice shook her head.

'You've never breathed a word of any of this. It's been like Melissa never existed.'

'It was a past I've been trying to leave behind. For Emmy's sake. You think I want her to know that her mother was a drug addict?'

'And you couldn't tell me because you thought I'd tell *her*?' Alice backed away. 'You really don't trust me, do you? I knew that. You said as much.'

'When? When did I ever say anything like that?'

'That day at work. When we agreed we had a problem. When I gave you the chance to tell me what you should have told me. What I had the right to know—that you knew damned well I'd never touched those drugs.'

'I said—'

'I *know* what you said, Andrew. And when I reminded you that you'd said you couldn't trust me, I saw you weighing it up. Deciding you still couldn't.'

'I wasn't even thinking about London. I was thinking about why I'd left. That I wanted to start again. To give Emmy a life with no shadows from the past.'

'And you thought I'd tell her,' Alice repeated. 'Or someone else. That the rumours would start all over again.'

The reason was there and it didn't help. It was only making things worse.

'You didn't trust me,' she whispered.

It didn't seem to matter what he said; it only seemed to be making things worse. But he couldn't stop. He was fighting for his future here. For his life.

'Of course I trust you. For God's sake, Alice—I

believed you when you told me you were on the pill and it was safe to have sex, didn't I?'

'Well, maybe I can't trust *you*.'

Andrew's jaw dropped. How had she switched the issue like that?

'You never told me the truth and it was *my* truth. *I'm* the one who had to suffer the suspicion. *I* was the one who couldn't get a job and lost my home and all my money. *I'm* the one who's been working here for years, hoping like hell nobody would ever find out why I had to leave my job in London.'

Alice's hands were moving as fast as the words were tumbling from her mouth. She unbuckled the halter on top of Ben's bridle and flipped the reins over his head. Then she was swinging herself up into the saddle.

'Not telling me was as good as lying to me. You don't trust me enough; that's what it boils down to.'

'And you just said you don't trust me,' he countered, still reeling from the attack. How on earth had things degenerated to this point? Accusations of mistrust. Of lying. Both of them hurting. The kind of pain he'd sworn to keep himself safe from, but here he was swimming in it.

Drowning in it.

'And it's true, isn't it? You've had your doubts? What about the day we were talking about your lease? I saw the way you flinched when all I did was clench a fist. I think you believed the rumours that I hit Mel. You looked horrified.'

'I was horrified by what I'd just said. I'm not into blackmail. I'm *not* Melissa.'

'No.' Andrew's breath came out in a huff of anger.

Man, this was pushing those old buttons. 'You'd have to be pregnant and expecting me to marry you to step into those shoes. I can't believe that you would think—'

The look on Alice's face stopped Andrew's words.

She looked...*stricken*.

And something clicked into place. The way she hadn't seemed to recover properly from that food poisoning episode.

Her nervousness.

The way she'd been avoiding him.

Good grief! She *was* pregnant!

Alice had to break that awful stare. The silence.

He had guessed. He *knew*.

She pulled on Ben's reins and kicked.

'No!' Andrew leapt forward and grabbed hold of the reins. 'What on earth do you think you're doing, Alice?'

She was escaping, that was all. Did he think it was dangerous to go riding because she was pregnant or something? She had to get away. She couldn't bear to have any further comparison made between herself and Melissa. She kicked harder and Ben tried to pull forward against Andrew's grip.

'You can't go,' Andrew said. Was that desperation in his voice? 'Please, Alice. I love you. Don't go.'

He *loved* her?

One tiny word, but the power it contained was immeasurable. If there was any way to be found out of this mess, that was where hope lay and it was all Alice needed to halt her bid to escape.

She tugged on the reins. The messages Ben was getting had now confused him completely but he tried to obey. He stopped and swung his head to look around at his mistress.

The movement pulled the reins from Andrew's hands and unbalanced him. And as Ben's head turned in one direction, his huge rump swung in the opposite direction.

Alice watched in horror as Andrew was sent flying. She saw his head hit the side of the concrete water trough.

And then she saw him lying, absolutely still, on the ground.

CHAPTER TEN

ANDREW lay, crumpled on one side. So still that Alice thought he must be dead.

With an anguished cry, she threw her leg over Ben's rump and slid to the ground with a bone-jarring thump. She pushed at her horse.

'*Move*, Ben! Get out of the way. Oh, *God*! What have we done?'

Dropping to her knees, so close to Andrew she was touching his back with her thighs, she bent over him.

Was he breathing?

Yes.

'Andrew? Can you hear me? Can you open your eyes?'

There was no movement on his face that she could discern. Alice placed trembling fingers on the side of his neck to feel for a pulse. She cupped the back of his head with her other hand and she could feel the warm stickiness of blood.

She'd seen him hit his head on the trough and now he was unconscious, with a head injury that could, potentially, be fatal.

The breath Alice had been unaware of holding came out in a sob. As carefully as she could, she examined his head without moving him. To have hit his head hard enough to knock him out meant there was a possibility of a neck injury as well. If she twisted his cervical spine, she could paralyse him for life. Or, worse, kill him. He was breathing and his pulse was steady and strong so there was no urgency to move him.

He was, in fact, lying in an almost perfect textbook recovery position. Alice slid her fingers through his hair, pressing onto his scalp to see if there were any spongy areas that could indicate a skull fracture. All she found, however, was the laceration that was bleeding copiously. She pressed her bare hand to the wound to try and control the bleeding with pressure.

With her other hand, she stroked his face. Touching his forehead and cheek and—very gently—his closed eyelids.

He *loved* her.

As much as this? Enough to feel that her life would be over if he wasn't alive and part of it any more?

He loved her and he trusted her. She *knew* that he trusted her. This whole confrontation had come about because of nothing more than her wounded pride. The fact that he hadn't told her why he believed she had been innocent of the charge of stealing drugs.

What did it matter?

She'd thought she'd been so hard done by, losing her job and that deposit on the apartment. Having to come home and start again, but it was nothing compared to what Andrew had gone through. Discovering the woman he'd married was a drug addict. Watching his helpless newborn suffering through withdrawal symptoms.

It would have torn him apart and, because of what made him the man Alice loved so much, he wouldn't have abandoned his marriage or Melissa. He would have done his utmost to help. To support her through any rehabilitation process. To pick up the pieces and try again. And again.

What was really amazing was that he'd believed in Alice enough to start a new relationship.

He had trusted her *that* much and she had just thrown it back in his face.

'I'm sorry,' Alice whispered. 'I'm so, so sorry.'

He'd come here, with Emmy, to start a whole new life. Of course he hadn't wanted to rake over such a miserable part of his past. They had agreed to leave it behind and she had been a more than willing accomplice.

If he'd told her about Melissa she would have wanted to know it all.

Now she did know it all and all she wanted to do was put it all behind them and start again.

'Please...' she heard herself say out loud.

Please let them have the chance to do exactly that.

'Please, Andrew. You have to be all right. I love you, too. I love you *so* much.'

Blinded by the tears filling her eyes, Alice didn't see the moment when Andrew's eyelids flickered open.

'I love *you*,' he said hoarsely.

'Ohh...' Alice blinked hard. She scrubbed at her face with her hand and tried to take in a deep breath. 'Don't move. You hit your head.'

'I'm okay.' But Andrew was frowning as he focused. 'You...you've got blood on your face.'

'Have I?' Automatically, Alice raised her hand to touch her face and then she realised why the blood was there. 'It's your blood,' she told Andrew. 'You've cut your head.'

His eyes drifted shut. 'You should have gloves on,' he murmured.

Alice's voice wobbled. 'I don't need them.'

She didn't. For the same reason they had known it was safe to have unprotected sex. The trust thing.

And she'd accused him of not trusting her.

She'd said she couldn't trust him because he'd lied to her.

Alice needed to ask Andrew questions to try and assess his condition but, for the moment, her throat was way too tight to allow her to utter a single word.

Andrew opened his eyes again. His voice was stronger this time.

'I love you, Alice Palmer.'

'I love you, too.'

Andrew smiled. 'Kiss me, then, babe.'

Alice bent down and touched his lips. Just a soft, brief press against her own. Andrew made a groaning sound as she lifted her head.

'Oh, God! Did I hurt you?'

'No.'

'What is it, then?'

'I needed a proper kiss.'

Something very close to laughter broke from Alice. 'What you need, my love, is an ambulance. A C collar. Probably an MRI scan of your head.'

'No.' Andrew's head moved in a side to side motion.

'Don't do that!' Alice pleaded. 'Stay still.'

'But I'm all right. I've just had a bump on the head and I'm feeling better all the time. I don't have any pain in my neck. I can wiggle all my fingers and toes, see?'

He demonstrated. 'Now, let me sit up.'

Reluctantly, Alice helped him into a sitting position and then watched him turn his head from one side to the other and then tilt it up and down.

'No pain,' he declared.

'What about your head?'

'That *is* a bit tender.' Andrew felt his scalp. 'Hmm. Good-sized egg, isn't it?'

'It's all my fault,' Alice said. 'I shouldn't have tried to ride away like that.'

'I shouldn't have been stupid enough to try and hang onto your reins. It's just as much my own fault. I'm sorry, Alice.'

'Not as sorry as I am.'

'I'm sorry I didn't try harder to find where you'd gone, back then. I knew it was wrong to leave things like that. I knew I'd only done enough to stop me feeling too guilty. I...was relieved I *didn't* find you.'

'Of course you were. You had more than enough to deal with in your life.'

'I didn't know, then, did I?'

Alice was confused. 'Know what?'

'That I would fall in love with you. Did I tell you that I love you?'

'Several times.' Alice gave him a thoughtful glance. 'Repetitive speech pattern. I think you've got a concussion.'

'I can prove my GCS is just fine. Ask me what day it is.'

Alice complied.

'It's the day I finally said what I should have said ages ago.'

'About Melissa?'

'No. That I love you.' Andrew moved and winced. 'Yes…about Melissa, too. I'll tell you anything you want to know. No more secrets.'

'I don't need to know anything else.'

'Don't you want to know how she did it? How she framed you so convincingly? The way she managed to bump into you that day and drop the ampoules right into your pocket?'

'Maybe later.' Strangely, Alice wasn't even curious at the moment. 'Right now, all I want to do is get you into the emergency department.'

'I'm fine.'

'I'm not going to believe that until someone who hasn't had a bang on the head tells me.'

'Don't call an ambulance.'

'Why not?'

'I don't need one and I certainly don't want one. How are you going to hold my hand if you're following behind in my car?'

'Your car?'

'We'll need to get Emmy. After you've been satisfied that I'm still functioning normally.'

'That's a point. I guess if I drive and you sit very still, it would be okay.' A tiny smile curled her lips. 'You really want me to hold your hand?'

Andrew tried to nod but it was clearly painful. He gripped her hand very tightly instead. 'Always,' he said fiercely. 'Don't let me go.'

'I won't,' she promised.

Alice helped him very slowly to his feet and it took a few minutes to make the careful journey to where he'd left his car.

'I'll go back and take Ben's tack off and put Jake inside,' Alice planned ahead aloud. 'Then I can take you into Emergency for observation and go and collect Emmy.'

'Alice?'

Andrew had stopped moving forward. The arm he had around Alice's shoulders tightened and she turned towards him.

'Are you all right? You're not feeling dizzy or sick or anything, are you?'

'I'm feeling...incredibly lucky.'

'Because you got knocked out? Hardly lucky.'

'Because you didn't ride away and leave me. That maybe I haven't left it too late to tell you I love you.'

'It's not too late, Andrew.'

'I wanted to tell you weeks ago. When you were sick. Before that, even, but...'

'I know.' Alice smiled into his eyes. 'It's huge and some things are too scary to say out loud. I wanted to tell you about the baby before this.'

'But you were scared because you thought I might think you'd planned it. Like Melissa did.'

Alice dropped her gaze as she nodded.

Andrew put a finger under her chin and tilted her face up again. She met his eyes and was instantly captured by the tenderness she could see. And the conviction.

'You're nothing like Mel,' Andrew told her softly. 'You never could be. You're you. So special and so wonderful that I love you more than I can ever hope to tell you. I never expected to find this. I thought Emmy was all I had in the world. All I needed.'

'Emmy is that special.' Alice smiled. 'I can understand that because I love her, too.'

'We're a family. Or we will be. Will you marry me, Alice?'

Alice smiled again and gently urged Andrew to keep walking towards his car.

'Ask me that again when you're not concussed.'

He did exactly that, as soon as the results of the CT scan Peter had insisted on came back showing no evidence of a significant head injury. Well after the wound had been cleaned and stitched.

Andrew waited only until Jo had gone, promising to fast-track his discharge summary.

'I'm not concussed,' he told Alice. 'Or only mildly. Enough to give me a headache for a day or two but not enough to undermine my judgement in any way.'

Alice couldn't resist teasing him a little. Perhaps because she knew what was coming and she wanted to draw this moment out for as long as she could to savour the delicious realisation of her dream.

'You're not supposed to drink alcohol or drive a car.'

'I'm not talking about driving a car.' Andrew caught hold of Alice's hand. 'I'm talking about what's going to drive the rest of my life.'

'Oh…' Alice let herself be drawn closer to where Andrew was sitting right on the edge of the bed. Tugged right between his legs, in fact.

Andrew raised her hand, turning it over so that he

could press a kiss to her palm. His gaze, however, remained locked with Alice's.

'I'm talking about you,' he said softly. 'The first, last and only woman I'm ever going to be in love with like this.'

Alice tried to swallow the lump that appeared like magic in her throat. She knew that conviction of having found 'the One'. She'd known that for her it was Andrew and she'd known that for many years. How unbelievable was it to be standing here, like this? Being touched by this man? Hearing him say the exact words she wanted to say to him?

'You and Emmy and our baby.' Andrew folded her even closer so that Alice's cheek rested against his and they were chest to chest. She could feel his heart beating against her own and she couldn't distinguish which pulse was hers. She didn't want to.

'We're a family, Alice. A perfect family.'

'Mmm.' The sound was a contented sigh.

'So...' Andrew pushed her back, just far enough to see her face properly '...will you marry me, Alice?'

'Yes.'

Such a tiny word but it came with a smile mixed with tears and it was all she needed to say, judging by the exquisite tenderness of the kiss Andrew bestowed on her.

A very brief kiss, because they were mindful of the fact that Jo would come rushing back any second now.

Sure enough, she came in, brandishing a pink slip of paper. She noted how close Alice was to Andrew and her smile broadened. She gave an approving nod as she handed over his clearance as a patient.

'You know what to watch out for,' she said to Alice. 'Any sign that we might have missed something.'

'You haven't,' Andrew assured her. 'I'm good to go.'

But when Jo left them to it, he didn't move.

'Shall we go?' Alice prompted.

'Not yet.'

'What about Emmy?'

'She's fine for a little while. She loves that after school play centre and I want to have another scan.'

'What?' Alice's heart skipped a beat. '*Why?* Is your headache worse? Vision blurry? Can't you—?'

Andrew pressed a finger to her lips. 'Not for me.' He was smiling. 'For you. For *us*.'

He could see she was still worried and his smile faded. 'You haven't forgotten Laura, have you? The threatened miscarriage?'

'Of course not. But…' Alice stopped and held her breath. This was important. As important as everything else Andrew had been saying since the accident.

'When I was giving her that scan to look for a foetal heartbeat, I had this image of it being us.'

Alice stared at him.

'Nothing to do with any complications,' Andrew added hurriedly. 'I was thinking in terms of an ordinary confirmation of pregnancy kind of scan. I wanted to be beside you. Holding your hand and waiting to see that little blip on the screen. I want to see it now. Our baby.'

So that was what that intense look had been about. The one that had been so overwhelming, given the secret she'd been keeping from Andrew.

Alice felt the prickle of unshed tears.

'Did I tell you that I love you?' she whispered.

Andrew feigned an innocent expression. 'I don't think I remember. I do have a mild concussion, you know. Tell me again.'

'Oh, I will, don't worry. You'll get sick of hearing it.'

'Never,' Andrew vowed and bent his head to kiss her again.

EPILOGUE

THE small girl had a very determined expression on her face.

She stood up tall in her stirrups and then sat down in the saddle. Up and down, in perfect time with the stride of her pony, as they went around in a small circle on a lush green paddock that was bathed by early summer sunshine.

'Perfect!' Alice called. 'You're posting, Emmy. Good girl!'

'Great stuff,' Andrew added, a proud grin on his face.

'You can stop now,' Alice told Emmy. 'Your legs must be getting tired.'

But Emmy kept going. Round and round, her face glowing with triumph.

Behind the fat, shaggy pony a large dog trotted. Riding shotgun to protect the child and keep her close to the rest of the family.

Leaning over the gate to this paddock was a huge black horse who looked as though he was dozing happily in the shade of the old tree but his ears flicked every time Paddington came nearer with his precious burden. He was watching just as closely as everyone else.

Alice stood with her back touching Andrew, who had his arms around her waist.

Or what used to be a waist. Currently, it was an impressive bulge. It was only a matter of weeks now until their son would be born.

'Daddy! Are you watching me? I'm *trotting!*'

'You sure are, darling. I'm very proud of you.'

His gentle hold on Alice tightened a little and the baby seemed to respond, moving beneath those loving hands. What an incredible sensation, being touched by people she loved from the inside and the outside at the same time. Alice let her breath out in a sigh.

'You okay?'

'I don't think I've ever felt this happy.'

'You're not missing being able to ride on such a gorgeous day?'

'Ben's enjoying his holiday and I'm way too busy to ride, anyway. There's still a way to go to get the garden into shape for the wedding.'

'It's too much work for you,' Andrew growled. 'What were we thinking, trying to get the restoration work on the house and garden done before we got married? We should have just skipped off to the nearest register office.'

'You know why.' Alice twisted a little so she could look up at Andrew's face. So that she could bask in the love she knew she would find there.

They'd decided to wait so that Emmy could be involved. Until after the baby was born. Because this wasn't just about a commitment ceremony between a man and a woman who loved each other so deeply.

It was to be a celebration of a new family.

And it would be Christmas time and they'd agreed that this was the most amazing gift anyone could ever give or receive.

A family.

'Look!' Emmy called. 'I can trot. Watch me, Mummy.'

Alice had to pull her gaze from Andrew's to look back at Emmy, but she was still within the circle of his arms.

'I'm watching, sweetheart.'

'So am I,' Andrew added.

They were. They would always watch over and love their children. And each other.

Because that was what families did.

MILLS & BOON

APRIL 2010 HARDBACK TITLES

ROMANCE

The Italian Duke's Virgin Mistress	Penny Jordan
The Billionaire's Housekeeper Mistress	Emma Darcy
Brooding Billionaire, Impoverished Princess	Robyn Donald
The Greek Tycoon's Achilles Heel	Lucy Gordon
Ruthless Russian, Lost Innocence	Chantelle Shaw
Tamed: The Barbarian King	Jennie Lucas
Master of the Desert	Susan Stephens
Italian Marriage: In Name Only	Kathryn Ross
One-Night Pregnancy	Lindsay Armstrong
Her Secret, His Love-Child	Tina Duncan
Accidentally the Sheikh's Wife	Barbara McMahon
Marrying the Scarred Sheikh	Barbara McMahon
Tough to Tame	Diana Palmer
Her Lone Cowboy	Donna Alward
Millionaire Dad's SOS	Ally Blake
One Small Miracle	Melissa James
Emergency Doctor and Cinderella	Melanie Milburne
City Surgeon, Small Town Miracle	Marion Lennox

HISTORICAL

Practical Widow to Passionate Mistress	Louise Allen
Major Westhaven's Unwilling Ward	Emily Bascom
Her Banished Lord	Carol Townend

MEDICAL™

The Nurse's Brooding Boss	Laura Iding
Bachelor Dad, Girl Next Door	Sharon Archer
A Baby for the Flying Doctor	Lucy Clark
Nurse, Nanny...Bride!	Alison Roberts

0310 Gen Std LP

MILLS & BOON

APRIL 2010 LARGE PRINT TITLES

ROMANCE

The Billionaire's Bride of Innocence	Miranda Lee
Dante: Claiming His Secret Love-Child	Sandra Marton
The Sheikh's Impatient Virgin	Kim Lawrence
His Forbidden Passion	Anne Mather
And the Bride Wore Red	Lucy Gordon
Her Desert Dream	Liz Fielding
Their Christmas Family Miracle	Caroline Anderson
Snowbound Bride-to-Be	Cara Colter

HISTORICAL

Compromised Miss	Anne O'Brien
The Wayward Governess	Joanna Fulford
Runaway Lady, Conquering Lord	Carol Townend

MEDICAL™

Italian Doctor, Dream Proposal	Margaret McDonagh
Wanted: A Father for her Twins	Emily Forbes
Bride on the Children's Ward	Lucy Clark
Marriage Reunited: Baby on the Way	Sharon Archer
The Rebel of Penhally Bay	Caroline Anderson
Marrying the Playboy Doctor	Laura Iding

0410 Gen Std HB

™MILLS & BOON®

MAY 2010 HARDBACK TITLES

ROMANCE

Virgin on Her Wedding Night	Lynne Graham
Blackwolf's Redemption	Sandra Marton
The Shy Bride	Lucy Monroe
Penniless and Purchased	Julia James
Powerful Boss, Prim Miss Jones	Cathy Williams
Forbidden: The Sheikh's Virgin	Trish Morey
Secretary by Day, Mistress by Night	Maggie Cox
Greek Tycoon, Wayward Wife	Sabrina Philips
The French Aristocrat's Baby	Christina Hollis
Majesty, Mistress...Missing Heir	Caitlin Crews
Beauty and the Reclusive Prince	Raye Morgan
Executive: Expecting Tiny Twins	Barbara Hannay
A Wedding at Leopard Tree Lodge	Liz Fielding
Three Times A Bridesmaid...	Nicola Marsh
The No. 1 Sheriff in Texas	Patricia Thayer
The Cattleman, The Baby and Me	Michelle Douglas
The Surgeon's Miracle	Caroline Anderson
Dr Di Angelo's Baby Bombshell	Janice Lynn

HISTORICAL

The Earl's Runaway Bride	Sarah Mallory
The Wayward Debutante	Sarah Elliott
The Laird's Captive Wife	Joanna Fulford

MEDICAL™

Newborn Needs a Dad	Dianne Drake
His Motherless Little Twins	Dianne Drake
Wedding Bells for the Village Nurse	Abigail Gordon
Her Long-Lost Husband	Josie Metcalfe

MILLS & BOON®

MAY 2010 LARGE PRINT TITLES

ROMANCE

Ruthless Magnate, Convenient Wife	Lynne Graham
The Prince's Chambermaid	Sharon Kendrick
The Virgin and His Majesty	Robyn Donald
Innocent Secretary...Accidentally Pregnant	Carol Marinelli
The Girl from Honeysuckle Farm	Jessica Steele
One Dance with the Cowboy	Donna Alward
The Daredevil Tycoon	Barbara McMahon
Hired: Sassy Assistant	Nina Harrington

HISTORICAL

Tall, Dark and Disreputable	Deb Marlowe
The Mistress of Hanover Square	Anne Herries
The Accidental Countess	Michelle Willingham

MEDICAL™

Country Midwife, Christmas Bride	Abigail Gordon
Greek Doctor: One Magical Christmas	Meredith Webber
Her Baby Out of the Blue	Alison Roberts
A Doctor, A Nurse: A Christmas Baby	Amy Andrews
Spanish Doctor, Pregnant Midwife	Anne Fraser
Expecting a Christmas Miracle	Laura Iding

millsandboon.co.uk Community

Join Us!

The Community is the perfect place to meet and chat to kindred spirits who love books and reading as much as you do, but it's also the place to:

- **Get the inside scoop from authors about their latest books**
- **Learn how to write a romance book with advice from our editors**
- **Help us to continue publishing the best in women's fiction**
- **Share your thoughts on the books we publish**
- **Befriend other users**

Forums: Interact with each other as well as authors, editors and a whole host of other users worldwide.

Blogs: Every registered community member has their own blog to tell the world what they're up to and what's on their mind.

Book Challenge: We're aiming to read 5,000 books and have joined forces with The Reading Agency in our inaugural Book Challenge.

Profile Page: Showcase yourself and keep a record of your recent community activity.

Social Networking: We've added buttons at the end of every post to share via digg, Facebook, Google, Yahoo, technorati and de.licio.us.

www.millsandboon.co.uk